Soccer
Shots

D1397603

By Werner Quies

Copyright © 1995
by Werner Quies

Soccer Shots

Quies, Werner.
   Soccer shots /by Werner Quies.
   p. cm.
   Preassigned LCCN: 95-60070
   ISBN 0-939116-37-5

   1. Soccer--Germany--Fiction. I. Title
   GV943.2.Q85 1995   796.334
                                QBI95-20015

Published by :   Frontier Publishing
                 P.O. Box 441
                 Seaside, OR 97138-0441
Cover Art by: Gary G. Savage

Printed in the United States of America

About the Author

Werner Quies, a native of Germany, is the director of Pacific Soccer School in Forest Grove, Oregon. He was a high school teacher for eighteen years.

Mr. Quies served as the first Director of Coaches and later as Director of Referees for the Oregon Youth Soccer Association. He holds the USSF "A" Licence and a coaching diploma from the German Soccer Federation.

The reunification of the two Germanies and the high hopes people held at that moment is the emotional and historical context of *Soccer Shots*. It is his second soccer novel for young adults.

Mr. Quies' first soccer fiction was published under the title of *The Incredible Soccer Story*. It tells the story of soccer great Pele's arrival in the United States and his impact on the game and its young players.

Mr. Quies holds a M.A. in comparative literature from the University of Oregon.

Foreword

Germany had been divided since 1945. The collapse of the Berlin Wall in 1989 signaled the reunification of East and West Germany.

Sixteen-year-old Karl Neumann, a fine soccer player, moves west to live with his aunt, uncle and a cousin, Rudi.

Karl's dream is to become a professional soccer player. This is the story of his struggle toward that goal and the related efforts to gain the support and acceptance of the people in the community of Feldhausen, his new home.

Acknowledgments

Vielen Dank! I give Special Thanks to my daughter, Erin, and son, Peter.

They injected the writing of *Soccer Shots* with the vital ingredients of any literary birth: enthusiasm, criticism, and superb ideas.

I express my gratitude to Charlie Graham and his fifth grade students at Dilley Elementary School — Thank you, my friends, your enthusiasm and perceptive feed-back helped me and inspired me.

Soccer Shots

Contents

 Soccer Shots

Dedication

To Bowie, Colt, Jody, Kenny, Larry, Lori, and Tony — my students, consultants, patient listeners, and friends.

I will always remember you.

1

Arrival in Feldhausen

"Uncle Wolfgang, can I give you a hand?" Karl asked.

"Hmm, let's see," Mr. Huber replied. "Have you ever cleaned a Mercedes before?"

Karl stared at his uncle's broad, hairy hand running a towel over the hood of the deep red luxury car. Then he slowly raised his head and met his uncle's eyes.

"Of course I haven't. I don't know of anyone back home in East Germany who owns such a fancy car." Karl's voice was tinged with annoyance. He took a step back and leaned against the garage wall.

"Don't take it so hard, Karl. My father is kind of fussy."

Karl heard his cousin's voice and saw a head pop up over the car's roof on the other side.

"But Rudi, tell me! What could I do wrong wiping dry the wheels, or a door, or the windows, or...?"

"Okay, okay. Listen!" Rudi cut in. He placed a rag on the car top and leaned forward. "This car is brand new, top of the line. We just got it today from the dealer before we picked you up at the train station in Frankfurt."

Karl took in a deep breath. His face relaxed. "I guess I kind of know how your dad feels. My mother is the same. She protects her possessions like a tigress guards her cubs. She has some cups, plates, and vases on shelves in the living room, stuff left to her by her grandmother. Mom never let me play soccer there. I guess she didn't have much trust in my shooting accuracy."

"Same here." Rudi had a smile on his face. "I only get to play soccer video games in my room. By the way, why don't you go up to the house and meet my mom. She is really excited to see you. It'll take us a while to finish here."

Karl nodded. *Great idea. Besides, I could use some fresh air.* He walked over to his belongings by the garage door, picked up his suitcase, tucked his soccer ball under his arm, and trudged out of the garage.

A brick-covered path, broken up by a few stepping stones, led Karl to the doorstep of the Huber villa. The huge house sat on top of a hill and looked intimidating in the dim light.

Karl sat down, rested his elbow on his suitcase, and looked around. In front of him rose a dark wall of giant evergreens. To his right, city lights illuminated the horizon. *That must be Feldhausen down there.*

Karl shivered in the cold, wet air. He crossed his arms tightly and tucked in his shoulders.

When he lowered his head, Karl's eyes fell on the label of his suitcase. He read his parents' name and address:

Walter und Anna Neumann
Strasse der Freiheit 89
Wittenberg
Deutsche Demokratische Republik

Street of Freedom, Democratic Republic. What a joke! A prison, nothing but a prison guarded by murderers. That's what my country is.

Then Karl's fingers glided over the label on his suitcase. Pictures and voices from home entered his mind. "It's up to you, son," he heard his mother's saying. "Your aunt and uncle invited you. I'll miss you a lot, but everyone says life is better in the West."

Then he saw himself sitting with his dad on the couch in the living room. His dad encouraged him, "Karl, you had excellent training here at the Kinder und Jugend Sportschule, but the opportunities are over there. Feldhausen is close to Eintracht, a great Bundesliga Club. Their scouts are always out and about looking for talent. You've got my blessings. Go for it!"

"We're almost done. Just the wheels are left to clean."

Rudi's yell ended Karl's daydream. He turned toward the garage. His eyes caught a glare of fiery

3

red and polished chrome. He winced and turned away.

Karl lowered his head. He saw that one of his tennis shoes, its canvas ripped and weathered, was untied. He grabbed both ends of the laces and pulled hard. Too hard! His right hand flew up and held a snapped shoe string.

Great start! Karl put his head into his hands. Weariness from a long day of traveling overpowered his body. Karl's head drooped forward and came to rest on the soccer ball in his lap. Then he fell asleep.

2

Aunt Gisela

A light came on and the front door opened. A woman stepped outside and, with arms flailing, caught herself. Looking down at her feet she discovered the gray pile that had almost made her tumble down the stairs.

"Mein Gott! Who do we have here?" she called out in surprise.

Karl stirred. He felt pressure on his shoulders. Then he heard a soft voice.

Karl raised his head and turned. He looked into a motherly face.

"Karl, nicht?" Mrs. Huber paused for a moment and Karl answered with a nod.

"I am your aunt, Aunt Gisela."

"Hi! Yes. I'm Karl Neumann. Thank you for asking me to come," he replied stiffly, shaking sleep from his head.

Mrs. Huber bent down and wrapped her arms around her nephew. "Come on, get up. You're going to catch a cold. Dinner is just about ready."

Karl dragged his heavy suitcase across the doorway.

"You and Rudi are sharing a room. It's back there, on the right." Mrs. Huber pointed toward the far end of the hallway.

The display over his cousin's desk pulled Karl closer. Ribbons, diplomas, pictures, and newspaper clippings all competed for space on the giant bulletin board. To the right, video cassettes and video games filled shelves reaching from top to bottom.

Wow, my cousin is a soccer player too! A big smile lit his face.

Rudi charged into the room. "Boy, what a team we've got, Karl!" he shouted, slapping his cousin on the shoulder with an open hand. "Still undefeated. We lead the league by three points."

"Looks like you have lots of players on your team," Karl said, pointing to Rudi's team picture.

"Yep. There are eighteen on our team, Fortuna Feldhausen."

Karl kept his eyes fixed on the photo. *Quite a few subs!*

"But Klaus, my best friend, is out for the season with a knee injury." Rudi put his finger on a tall blond player in the middle of the photograph.

"Uhh, then you need another ..." Karl could not finish his remark as his cousin kept on talking.

"Next to him, on the left, the big husky guy is Bruno, the coach's son."

"Mean-looking kid — with that big frown," Karl interjected.

"Right on, Karl. Bruno's feet are cannons. He also tackles like one of those hulks in American Football. We call him 'The Enforcer.' I am learning a lot from him," Rudi added with a short laugh.

"You've got his build, Rudi. But I don't think it matters a lot in soccer."

"Just wait and you'll see. Hardly any forward gets close to him. They turn and dribble toward their own goal when they see Bruno rushing at them." Rudi broke out into a boisterous laugh.

Karl waited for Rudi to calm down. "Nice uniforms you're wearing. Jerseys, shorts, socks, almost blood red. Just like the Devils from the Betzenberg."

"Exactly, and we got a prominent sponsor just like the team from Kaiserslautern." Rudi referred to one of the clubs playing in the Bundesliga, the West German Professional Soccer League.

"Sponsor? What are they doing for your team?"

"Umbrella Insurance, my dad's company, pays a lot of our bills. And they're going to pay our way to Italy to watch the Soccer World Cup in June."

"Really?" Karl raised his eyebrows.

"Sure. That's going to be our reward for winning the championship."

"The championship? But it's only November and the season is only a few months old." Karl looked bewildered.

"So what?" Rudi snickered. "There's no one who can beat us."

In sports anything is possible. Pictures of

famous upsets in the world of athletic competition flashed through Karl's mind.

Then he looked up into his cousin's eyes and said, "Rudi, did you know that I play soccer too?"

"Well, yes. I saw you coming with a soccer ball. When you got off the train you held it like a mother holds a baby in her arms."

"Look, this is my soccer ball." Karl went over to his bed and picked up his ball. "Actually, it was my brother's ball. He gave it to me as a good-bye present." Karl stroked the worn and scarred leather.

"What an old, strange-looking ball," Rudi exclaimed. "We use Adidas World Cup balls in our club."

Karl grimaced. "Do you want to know what happened to my brother?" he asked weakly.

"Yeah, okay, tell me. Martin, right?"

"Yes, that's my brother's name."

"My mother talked about him a long time ago," Rudi said. "Didn't he climb over the Berlin Wall?"

"No, not quite, Rudi," Karl replied softly. He squeezed his eyes shut against his tears. Then he turned to his suitcase at the foot of his bed.

"What in the world do you have in there?" his cousin shouted. "It's a rock, a concrete block. What is it for?" Rudi looked dumbfounded.

"It's a piece of the Berlin Wall. I call it my 'Martin Rock.' I chiseled it out of the Wall, from the spot where they shot my brother." Karl wiped away some tears.

"Oh, my God! That's awful!" stammered Rudi. "But why, why was he shot?"

"He was shot by a border guard. Martin wanted to get across to the other side, that's all."

"From East Berlin to West Berlin?"

Karl nodded his head. "Martin bled to death at the foot of this damned wall." He raised his voice and sighed. "Rudi, come close. Look at these red signs; here, part of a circle."

Rudi took the rock into his hands. "Graffiti, maybe part of the Peace Symbol."

"The Peace Symbol, you think?" Karl shuddered. Irony had struck him with full force.

"Sure. Why not?" Rudi replied. "People painted all kinds of stuff on the Wall, didn't they?"

"Yeah, sure. I saw it. I saw that Concrete Monster, early this morning."

"What? Just today?" Rudi had his mouth wide open.

Karl nodded. "Exactly at ten-thirty in the morning, Thursday, November 9, 1989, I walked through the Berlin Wall."

"You did? Of course, I saw it on TV. But I didn't know you were among them."

"I certainly was!" Karl said emphatically. "They just let us through, thousands of people."

"You mean, your brother was shot to death...and now anybody just goes...." Rudi was groping for words. "I don't get it."

"I don't think anybody does." Karl looked into his cousin's eyes. "Rudi, do you think I could put my rock and my soccer ball, the two together, on your shelf up there?"

"Sure, why not?" Rudi answered hesitatingly. "I guess I can move my trophies and my video games closer together."

3

Recollections

Karl and Rudi had shifted things around on the trophy shelf when Mrs. Huber entered the room. "Dinner is on the table. Schnitzel, fried potatoes, red cabbage. Cheesecake for dessert," she announced with a smile.

Rudi dashed toward the dining-room as if on a break-away for the winning goal.

"Hold it! Not so fast!" Mrs. Huber caught her son by the arm. "Let me have a quick look at both of you."

Mrs. Huber moved her eyes back and forth between her son and her nephew. "How much you look alike!" she exclaimed. "The hair, bushy and chestnut-colored, the dark, devilish eyes. And those freckles! You must have the same amount." Karl noticed the smile in his aunt's eyes.

"What do you mean by 'looking so much alike'"? Rudi protested. "Karl looks at least two years younger than I do."

"True. Karl might seem a little younger than you. But he is your age." Mrs. Huber scolded Rudi with a stern look for his tone of voice.

11

"Really?"

"Yes, Rudi. Karl's mother and I are twins. With a little luck, you and Karl would have become 'twin cousins.' You were born only four days apart, sixteen years ago."

Rudi finally struggled free. Mrs. Huber took a step toward Karl and took her nephew by the hand. "Come on. Let's go and eat. I've already put the dinner on the table."

Karl lay in bed. It was late in the evening of the day of his arrival. His mind was full and so was his stomach.

Pictures from his eventful day whirled through his head. He saw himself waving good-bye to his parents at the Wittenberg train station.

Then Karl again felt the hurt when first meeting his uncle in Frankfurt. "So, here is our boy from East Germany, our 'little Ossi,'" his uncle had greeted him handing him a banana. "Go ahead, eat it now. You've probably never had one before."

My uncle sure acts like a brute. Maybe he doesn't like me. I wonder why. I need to talk to Aunt Gisela about this.

At the thought of his aunt a wave of warmth washed over him. Her voice and soft eyes reminded Karl of his mother. *And what a meal we had tonight! What a cook she is!* Then another thought troubled him. *Why didn't my aunt say anything about my height or my skinny body?*

Rudi is right. We don't look alike. I am at least half a head shorter than he is. And Rudi's stomach and chest! Huge! What an enormous pair of thighs! Rudi must be thirty pounds heavier than I am!

Karl's eyes searched for his soccer ball and Martin Rock on the shelf. Shafts of light entering through the blinds gave shape to his two prized possessions.

From across the room he heard Rudi take deep breaths.

Karl wasn't sure whether or not his cousin was already asleep. "Rudi! Rudi!" Karl's hushed but urgent voice did not draw a response. All evening a question had been burning in Karl's heart. *Can I be on your soccer team?* Somehow the time just had not been right.

4

Locked Gates

Darkness still blanketed the room when Karl woke up and jumped out of bed. He fell on hands and knees, groped for his suitcase and raised the lid. Karl searched for his training gear.

First he got a hold of his sweat suit. His fingers could have located any grass stain or dirt spot on it in the dark. On the back of his red sweat jacket he visualized the bold black letters of LOKOMOTIVE underneath the emblem of a steam engine. They were the name and logo of his East German soccer team.

In a few short minutes he was dressed. Karl zipped his jacket and threw a last glance in the direction of his ball and Martin Rock. Then he quietly headed for the front door and stepped into the cold morning.

The city lights were a magnet pulling him downhill. His tennis shoes crushed thin layers of ice. A thin veil of steam from his breath disappeared in the fog. Karl could not see further than the next tree, the next house, or the hedge along the walkway. But he paid little attention to his

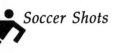

surroundings. Following the path, he charged ahead.

Karl entered Feldhausen. His legs carried him through the business section with its two restaurants, the butcher shop, and the bakery. Then, uphill into a wall of darkness, Karl chased his gradually disappearing shadow.

The fading city lights revealed an opening to the right. It tempted him to enter. Soon a thicket of small trees on either side of the narrow trail swallowed him. There were no more lights to pull him ahead. Now it was the locomotive on his back that pushed Karl further and further into unknown territory.

Karl was on a winding incline when a tree root caught his foot and threw him headlong to the ground. He cried out in pain.

Slowly he sat up and touched his face. His hand felt blood trickling down his lips. *Where am I? What am I doing here?* He gazed about him as if he were on another planet.

Slowly, Karl became fully aware of his situation. He was sitting in darkness on a narrow trail many miles away from his cousin's home. He swallowed some blood mixed with sweat when a thought electrified him. *The soccer field! Where is the small stadium I saw on the photo last night?*

Charged with new energy, Karl jumped to his feet and ran downhill, the way he had come. In the valley a small creek joined him in his dash east toward dawn's early light.

FORTUNA STADIUM. A wooden sign on a tree pointed to the right. With each step the horizon took on clearer outlines. The giant spider web which had filled his vision turned into a mesh wire fence. Karl had reached the stadium entrance.

A pleasant picture painted itself in his mind. He would enter through the gate. Then the lush turf would challenge him to spend the last of his energy in some dashes across the field.

There was the entrance. Karl pushed on the gate. It didn't budge. His heart jumped when his eyes fell on a heavy chain and a padlock. "No! But why?" he yelled, rattling the door violently. "There must be an open gate somewhere!"

In a few minutes Karl was back at the same spot. A sprint around the stadium, his eyes glued to the wire, had revealed the fact that this was the only entrance.

Karl leaned forward with both hands on the gate. He sucked in deep puffs of air and stared at the playing field. Shrouds of fog rose from the roof of the bleachers. Near him a strip of turf sparkled with the reflection of the first rays of the rising sun.

What can I do to get in? Trying to find an answer in the sky, he raised his head. A sign above the gate arrested his eyes: ENTRANCE FOR MEMBERS AND TICKET HOLDERS ONLY.

Members only! Strange. Just like in East Germany! But my aunt will help me. Maybe even my

17

uncle. It shouldn't be difficult to become a member and then get on the field.

These thoughts put life back into his body. Karl turned away from the fence and headed for home.

5

A Burning Question

The Huber home welcomed Karl with the enticing aroma of freshly brewed coffee. *Is it Christmas already?* Karl knew that it was only on the most special occasions that his mother had made "real coffee."

However, it was a very ordinary Friday morning that found Karl's aunt in the kitchen. Fashioned in the mold of the traditional German Hausfrau she did not neglect her family's stomachs.

Karl felt his eyes bulge. He had never seen such piles of cold cuts, cheeses, rolls, breads, and cakes.

"Mein Gott! Where have you been?" Mrs. Huber exclaimed. She had turned away from the stove when she heard her nephew enter the kitchen. Karl saw the glare in her eyes. He felt the concern and reproach on her face.

"I have been worried to death. A little longer and I would have called the police."

Karl shrank from the tongue-lashing. "I'm sorry, Aunt Gisela. I got lost. I should have told

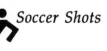

you last night that I always get up early to run."

Mrs. Huber's face softened. "Go ahead, sit down. Tell me about your early morning adventure."

Rudi entered. He had abandoned his bed at the scents of breakfast. He sat down across from his cousin and listened. "You do all that running in the middle of the night?" Rudi called out in a flippant tone of voice.

"Middle of the night?"

"Well, practically, Karl. And with an empty stomach on top of it. What for?"

"It's part of my training program. A coach at the Kinder und Jugend Sportschule in East Germany designed it especially for me."

"A soccer training program designed just for you?" Rudi echoed in disbelief.

"Yes. That's what KJS did for promising athletes."

"So, why didn't you stay over there? It sounds like you had it made."

"No, Rudi. They bossed me around all the time. I couldn't do what I or my parents wanted. I was not allowed to go anywhere. They tried to do the same thing to Martin. Besides, I want to play soccer here, professionally, in the BUNDESLIGA."

"Wow, you're quite a dreamer!"

"I guess I am. But I'll do it!"

Karl and Rudi ate in silence for a short while. Then Rudi's head shot up. While chewing on a cheese sandwich he said excitedly, " Karl, listen. Last night on TV, they talked about the possibility of East and West Germany unifying soon. It's also going to happen in the Bundesliga. There will be some teams from the East joining the Pro League here in the West."

Karl nodded. "I think you're right, Rudi. Lots of things will get better in my country once the two Germanies are back together again. But I sure don't want to sit around for a few years and wait till they're going to get things straightened out in the East."

In the breakfast-eating competition that morning Karl and Rudi settled for a tie. Karl swallowed the last bite of a ham sandwich. He looked up from his plate and asked Rudi, "Do you know how I can get into the stadium for my next workout?"

Rudi shook his head. "There's no way. Hardly anyone is allowed on the field. They try to keep it in top shape for all League Games. Once in a great while Coach Meierbär makes an exception."

"How about your father, can he get me in?"

"Well, yes. He has a key. But..."

"So, we could borrow the key, get in, and practice shooting together, couldn't we?" Karl asked hopefully.

"I don't think he'll let us. Besides, I never have time, with homework and playing soccer video games."

Karl looked at his cousin open-mouthed. *How can sitting in a room and pushing buttons be more exciting than roaming around on a soccer field?*

"Hmm, I just remembered," Rudi broke the

silence. "Next Thursday it's going to be different. Last..."

"What do you mean? What's going to be different?" Karl interrupted.

"Just wait, I'll tell you!" his cousin shot back. "Last practice before the winter break. Kind of a reward. Meierbär is going to open the stadium gate. Turn on the lights. Party afterwards."

"You're having a soccer practice next Thursday?" Karl pushed his head half-way across the table toward Rudi.

"Sure, we practice every Thursday. Starting next week we'll take a break until February. Too much rain, snow, and cold coming up."

"I see. And next week, do you think I could...?"

"Could what?" Rudi raised his voice. He must have felt the burning in Karl's eyes.

"Rudi, do you think I could practice with you guys next week?"

"Well, maybe. Just don't know." Rudi shrugged his shoulders.

"I can play, Rudi. I'll contribute." Karl pleaded with his eyes.

""Okay. I'll talk to my dad. He's good friends with the coach."

"Thanks, Rudi. When do you think you can ask him?"

"At noon, I guess. He is down at the 'Golden Duck,' our club restaurant. They're making plans for our Italy trip." Rudi paused for a moment. Then he spoke up again, betraying a touch of anger. "What's the big deal? Why are you so nuts about practicing, playing, the stadium?"

Karl closed his eyes searching for an answer. His reply came slowly. "Rudi, I told you already." "Yeah, you sure did. I remember. Of course, I like to play soccer, too. But I would hate to chase a ball around all week long. That's what you would have to do as a pro. Besides, my dad knows how I can make money without killing myself running around."

It was Karl's bed that decided his activities for the rest of the morning. While Rudi headed to his side of the room looking for his favorite video game, Karl became easy prey for gravity and a soft mattress. His long run and the long train ride the day before were starting to take their toll. He lay down and dozed off quickly.

6

Mr. Huber

Late in the afternoon Karl woke to sounds of Rudi's video game. Looking at his cousin's broad back and his motionless posture, Karl thought that Rudi resembled a Buddha statue.

From the living room next door escaped the muffled sounds of clapping hands and the soft 'pob,' 'pob' of tennis rackets striking a ball. *My uncle must be back. He's watching the Davis Cup Final between West Germany and Sweden.*

Karl sat up in his bed and called in the direction of his cousin. "Hey, Rudi. Could you talk to your father now?"

Rudi did not move. Karl got up and moved over to his cousin. Reaching for his shoulder, Karl repeated his question.

"Talk about what?" Rudi replied, not taking his eyes off the screen. His fingers frantically jumped about the keyboard.

"You know, your soccer team. Thursday's practice."

"Oh yeah, I remember."

"So, could you ask him now, please?"

"He's right next door. Ask him yourself. I've got to destroy the next wave of aliens."

Karl sat down on his bed. He felt fear in his stomach. *My uncle is bound to chew me out.* Karl's eyes wandered around the room. They came to rest on his ball. Karl closed his eyes and started to daydream. He saw himself with Martin in the backyard of their house. He was a tiny first grader and Martin a tall fourteen-year-old. Rose-bushes were in bloom along the east side of their yard. Opposite, some thirty yards across, stood a long hedge of evergreen his parents had planted. Connected to the hedge was a sturdy wooden fence the height of a soccer goal.

Karl saw himself and his brother dribbling, taking shots at each other, playing for hours until their mother called for the fifth time," Dinner is ready."

"Now, keep your ankle locked. Hit through the ball," Karl could hear Martin speak to him. Then his brother would take Karl's foot, point his toes down, and make it strike the ball, again and again. Later on, goal-keepers found out that Karl had the powerful shot of a grown-up.

Karl opened his eyes. They flashed with determination. He looked at his ball and the rock on the shelf. *I'll talk to my uncle now!* Karl jumped out of bed and headed for the living room.

"Sit down, Ossi," his uncle welcomed him, pointing to the space next to him on the couch.

"My name is not Ossi, Uncle."

"Come on, don't be so touchy. Everybody from the East is an 'Ossi' here."

Karl swallowed a reply and sat down.

"Here, look! Do you see how Boris is beating up on this Swedish kid? This is the way our Fortuna team plays soccer. Aggressive, gutsy, not giving the other guy a chance to breathe," Mr. Huber spouted excitedly.

Karl's eyes followed the ball moving from Boris Becker to Stefan Edberg, back and forth. After a few minutes Karl cleared his throat and said, "Uncle Wolfgang, can I ask you something?"

"You want to know how we get players like Boris or Steffi Graf, or Rudi Voeller. Let me..."

"No, I want to....," Karl tried to break in.

"Let me tell you something," his uncle continued, ignoring Karl's interruption. "As far as tennis and soccer are concerned, just to mention these two, you guys in East Germany are still way back. Yes, light-years behind in..."

"No, Uncle! Please listen to me! I want to talk to you about playing on Rudi's team," Karl pleaded with force.

Mr. Huber stopped dead in his tracks. He looked up slowly. His eyes glowered.

Karl held up under the weight of his uncle's glare.

"Do you think I could play on Rudi's team?" Karl asked again. His voice was strong and polite.

Mr. Huber reached for his bottle of Heninger Bier and refilled his glass.

His eyes had softened and his words came with surprising calm.

"Well, let's see. I have heard that you can play. Way back, your mother wrote something about you becoming quite a star. Your brother Martin, too. I guess he was, poor guy."

Karl sat quietly, his head nodding and his eyes fixed on his uncle.

"I know Meierbär well. He is Fortuna's coach." Mr. Huber stopped and looked up at the ceiling. He seemed to grope for words.

"Of course, I can't promise anything. They have an injury and Meierbär is looking.."

"I know, Klaus. He is injured. Rudi told me about it last night." Karl could not hide his excitement.

"Well, yes, but...." Mr. Huber's reply was drawn out.

Karl felt Mr. Huber's doubt. "Uncle, tell me what's wrong," he pleaded.

"I'll talk to Meierbär about you. My thoughts might be wrong. All I can say is that the Fortuna coach is known for fielding teams with powerful, strong athletes."

Karl's face dropped. He felt the full force of the message.

He can't be serious. I can play! Pierre Littbarski, Thomas Haessler. They are small. They are quick. They have skills. They can play!

Karl crawled back into his room and crashed on his bed. Rudi didn't notice him. He still sat among his high-tech gadgets. Lost in his world of life on a screen, he could have set a new world record impersonating a Buddha in trance.

Karl stared out the window. The dreary November evening didn't hold much promise for exciting events to happen.

7

Nightmare

Karl, above all, be patient. He remembered one of his father's words of advice. Still, images of things that had gone wrong way back passed before his eyes: there was the day in school when he flunked his Russian language test and coiled under his teacher's verbal thrashing, then he saw himself sitting behind his dad's workshop with his last girlfriend's letter in his hands. She had informed him that "she needed to cool off their relationship."

Karl twisted and turned. He pounded his pillow as if to force the demons of bad news out of his head. Finally, the struggle on the outside stopped; he fell asleep.

But right away a horrible nightmare had him in its grip. Karl saw himself sitting in a ghost-train. His hands clutched on to the narrow windowsill. The train charged through a house. A shriek of terror crushed his eardrums. It came from a woman. With her mouth wide open, she stood in the kitchen by the phone. The deathly mask screaming *N-E-I-N* was his mother. Someone

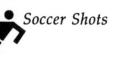

was telling her that her oldest son had been killed.

The ghost-train swung around a corner. Karl saw his brother desperately trying to scale a wall. A giant hand smashed him to the ground. A fountain of blood exploded from his brother's chest, smearing the wall with red.

Around the next bend, an ocean of crosses plunged upon him. The train sped through a cemetery toward an open grave. Karl wanted to scream when the train approached the pitch-black abyss. Then, the train slowed down. He got off the train.

Karl saw himself standing by a grave. He looked miserable in a drab, ill-fitting suit. People in black, women and men in tears, surrounded him. Karl dug into a pile of dirt, filled the shovel, and tossed the earth down onto his brother's coffin. The heavy thud of the soil striking the black wood woke him.

"Mein Gott, was ist los? You're soaked in sweat!" Mrs. Huber exclaimed. She had a towel in her hand and wiped Karl's face and forehead dry. "I think I'll call Dr. Himmlich."

Karl smiled weakly. "No, Aunt Gisela, I'll be all right."

"Are you sure? You certainly do have a temperature."

"I'll be fine in a few minutes. I just had a bad dream." He told his aunt what he had experienced.

Mrs. Huber listened in silence, biting her lips.

"Of course, I know what happened to your brother. The pain never goes away, does it?"

"No. It's just as though it only happened yesterday," Karl replied.

"And your mother? How is she doing? She can't forget, can she?"

"I don't think so. She doesn't smile any more the way she used to."

"Why did Martin risk his life trying to escape?" his aunt asked after a long pause.

"Martin was a very good soccer player. Government people took care of him. They told him to practice, where, when, how often, how hard. But he just couldn't do some things they asked him to."

"Like what?" his aunt wanted to know.

"Going to meetings. Saying stuff he didn't believe. Things like that."

"I think I understand," his aunt replied. "I know people in East Germany were not free to plan and live their own lives."

Karl nodded. "I remember my brother's last words to me. He woke me up very early one morning. My room was dark. 'Karl, I must go now. I want to be free. I want to play in the West. Some day our country will be without walls and watch towers. Then I'll see you again.' He gave me his ball and left."

Karl leaned back and rested his head on the pillow. He breathed in deeply. "Aunt, I'll do it for Martin." Karl snapped forward and grabbed his aunt by the arm. "Can you help me to get on Rudi's team?"

"Oh, sure. That shouldn't be a problem."

"Really?"

"I don't see why? I'll talk to your uncle. He has connections. I'm sure they can use a good player."

"I hope so," Karl replied.

"And I'll make you a cup of tea, a nice cup of hot herb tea with lemon and honey. And a piece of cake. We still have some of the cheesecake you like so much."

Smiling now, Karl watched his aunt leave the room.

8

Monika

Karl was up and running early the next morning. He did not get very far. Turning right at the very first intersection, a violent blow sent him sprawling onto the road. He heard shrieks and the screech of metal scraping asphalt.

"Help, help!" a voice cried from across the street. Whimpers followed.

Karl stood up and limped toward the voice. His hand tested his ribs, shoulder, and right knee. Everywhere his body cried out in pain.

"Just bruises, I hope," he whispered.

Karl moved across the sidewalk to where the street light fell on a pair of white Adidas tennis shoes and blue sweat pants. A little to the left lay a bicycle.

Suddenly, Karl was wide awake. Many hours of First Aid training in East Germany had prepared him to deal confidently with the situation on hand.

"Keep calm. Don't move. I'll help you," he shouted.

A deep moan greeted him when he looked into

the face of a girl about his own age. Wide eyes stared at him. Karl searched for the girl's hand and held it tight. He saw the fear gradually drain from her face.

"No head or neck injuries, no spine problems, no breaks," Karl exclaimed after a cursory examination. "You'll be all right. Just a few scrapes and bruises and a tear in your sweat pants."

The girl returned Karl's smile. Soon he had learned that her name was Monika Sanchez.

"I should have opened my eyes turning that corner," he said.

"No, it was my fault. I'm sorry." Monika spoke with a slight accent.

"Well, actually you had the right of way," Karl replied, pointing to the stop sign at the intersection.

Monika laughed and straightened herself. Long black hair fell in disarray around her shoulders. Karl saw that she was a little shaky on her legs and felt that she was very much in need of his support. He took her by the arm, and they turned around to examine Monika's bike.

"Wow, what a bike! A Bianchi!"

"Yes, a birthday gift from my parents. I hope it's not broken."

"Let's see." Karl examined the bike. "Putting the chain back on the sprocket is a cinch, like scoring on a penalty kick. But the derailleur cable..."

"Is it bad?" Monika interrupted with concern.

"No, not really. The derailleur cable broke off from the gear shift lever. I'll need tools to fix it."

"You'll be able to repair it?" Monika asked surprised.

"Sure. My dad and I used to put bikes together from scratch. We even built a rototiller. We collected pieces here and there over the years."

"You did?" Monika was surprised.

"You see, I grew up in East Germany."

"Oh, now I understand. Things are very difficult to get there, right?"

"Yeah, tell me about it. It takes about ten years to get a car. And it's always a lousy one, on top of it."

Karl felt Monika's admiring glance as they headed, bike in tow, towards the Huber residence.

Karl had not exaggerated. With the tools he found in his uncle's garage, Monika's bike was soon back in riding condition.

"I'm getting ready for a tennis tournament next week in Frankfurt," Monika replied when Karl asked her why she was riding her bike so early.

"Oh, you're a tennis player," Karl exclaimed. "That's a great sport. You must be good; you look like an athlete."

Monika blushed slightly. "I don't know, but I work hard at it. Tennis is a lot of fun."

Karl looked at Monika. He took in her big dark eyes. *She could, with those blackberry eyes of hers, make any referee change calls against her. And that accent, I bet she is from some exotic southern country.*

"No, I'm a 'Bundi'; I was born in the Bundesrepublik," she said laughing when Karl asked her about her place of birth. "But my father is Spanish."

"That's what I suspected," Karl said. "My mother is German, and I like sauerkraut and frankfurters better than paella."

They both laughed.

Monika prepared to leave. She took her bike by the handlebars. "Karl, can you give me your phone number? I might need your help again when I run someone else over."

"There are two fours and a seven. At the end there is a zero, but I'm not sure," Karl stammered.

"Why won't you give me your phone number?" Monika asked in mock surprise.

"No, that's not it," Karl protested.

"Well, what's the reason?"

"I don't remember it. I just moved in here the day before yesterday." Karl told Monika more about his situation and about his soccer ambitions.

"Oh, I see. Great! You're a soccer player and your uncle is Wolfgang Huber."

"You know him?"

"Of course. He is Mr. Soccer around here. Always in the paper. And his son Rudi, too."

"You know Rudi?"

"Not really. My brother Carlos plays against him sometimes."

"You have a brother? He plays soccer?" Karl's head shot up.

"Oh, you'll bet he does! Carlos is almost seventeen and he is crazy about soccer. He plays goalie for Germania Burgholz."

"Germania Burgholz?"

"Yes. Burgholz is where I live. His team is pretty good. They are only three points behind Fortuna."

"Now I remember," Karl replied. "Rudi talked about Germania. He said that they were in second place."

Monika nodded and pushed her bike out of the garage.

"Monika," Karl shouted, running after her and grabbing her by the arm. "Wait a minute, I'll get paper and a pencil. I'm afraid you might not have another accident very soon."

For a long time Karl stood rooted to the garage floor. One hand traced the pain in between his ribs. The other hand clutched his new treasure: a name, an address, and a phone number scribbled on a discarded envelope.

9

Good News

"Good morning, Karl," his aunt greeted him in the kitchen after Karl had showered and dressed. "Did you have a good run?"

"Well, I didn't get very far today. Just one block."

Mrs. Huber had a puzzled look on her face. Too busy with her breakfast preparations, she didn't notice the additions to Karl's scratches and light cuts on his left cheek and forehead.

"One block? I don't understand."

"I had another accident. But it was the best crash I ever had in my life." Karl smiled and proceeded to tell his aunt about running into Monika.

"Monika Sanchez? Really!" his aunt exclaimed. "She's well known. A fine tennis player. Maybe the next Steffi Graf." Mrs. Huber paused for a moment. "Well, tell me, how do you like her?"

She didn't get an answer. Karl's face was an open book. He could not suppress a radiant smile.

Mrs. Huber changed the subject. "Your uncle

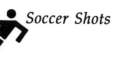

and cousin have already left. My husband drops Rudi off at school on his way to work."

"School," Karl groaned, sitting down for breakfast. "Do I have to go there too?"

"Definitely," his aunt replied. "We'll enroll you this week. But you don't have to attend classes until after Christmas break."

"Great, a few more weeks of freedom!"

"It sounds like you didn't like school in Wittenberg."

"Not really. I hate history. All that communist propaganda. And Russian. What a bear!"

"Oh, yes, Russian. I forgot. Here you have to study English. We'll have to get you a tutor so you can catch up."

"I'd rather learn Spanish. I think I might know of the perfect teacher." Karl had a grin on his face and his aunt wore a knowing smile.

Karl swallowed a sip of warm milk and put down his cup. "Aunt, by the way, did you talk to Uncle Wolfgang about my playing soccer for Fortuna?"

"Oh, yes. Late last night. I was just about to tell you. My husband talked to the coach on the phone, right away."

"What did Coach Meierbär say?" Karl asked eagerly.

Mrs. Huber was slow to respond. "He mentioned to your uncle that they had plenty of players. But he wants to see you, nevertheless."

"See me play?"

"I assume so. You are supposed to go with Rudi on Thursday."

Karl did not notice his aunt's guarded optimism. Jumping up from his chair, he exclaimed, "Super! I'll get ready for a workout right now."

"It can't be much fun practicing by yourself, can it?" his aunt wondered.

"It's okay. I'm going to work on shooting today. Shots over a wall of defenders. That was Martin's specialty. I'm going to be as good as my brother."

"Rudi thinks one can improve soccer skills playing video games. Don't you want to give it a try? It's so cold outside."

"No way, Aunt." Karl laughed. "My legs won't get stronger and my shooting won't get more accurate by pecking buttons."

"I think you're right, Karl," his aunt replied, nodding. "That's Rudi's excuse to be lazy."

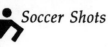

10

Welcome Money

Back in his room Karl opened a drawer and took out clothes for his next workout: socks, shorts, T-shirt, sweats. Then, his heart fell. He realized that the tennis shoes he wore were the only shoes he had. *I can't practice with these flimsy things!* Karl hit his forehead with the palm of his hand. *I need soccer shoes — a pair of good soccer shoes.*

Karl went to his suitcase in the closet and dug for his wallet. There it was. He pulled out some bank notes — five East German 100 Mark bills.

A minute later he was in the kitchen talking to his aunt about buying a pair of soccer shoes.

"You have five hundred East German Mark," his aunt said looking at one of the bills. "Do you know what the exchange rate is, Karl?"

"Not really, I know our East German money is worth a lot less."

"You're right. For this bill the bank will give you nine or ten Mark of our money." Mrs. Huber waved one of Karl's 100 Mark bills.

"Aunt, that can't be possible," Karl stam-

mered. His face was as white as the chalk mark-
ings on a soccer field. "I'll only get about fifty
Mark for all of my money?"

"The rate is changing almost daily right now,"
his aunt replied. "In a month or two, or after the
reunification of the two Germanies, you might get
much more."

"But I need soccer shoes now," Karl said
dejectedly.

"At the present rate of exchange your money
will buy you only one shoe, not a pair." Mrs.
Huber pressed her lips together tightly, not in-
tending to make a joke.

Karl sat down. His shoulders dropped. His
aunt hurried around the table and put an arm
around his shoulder. "I know it's not fair. Unfor-
tunately, that's the way it is," she tried to console
him.

"Aunt, do you know that this is all the savings
I have?" Karl's voice was filled with anger. "I
repaired bikes and did odd jobs. I worked every
day after school before soccer practice."

"I believe it." She pulled Karl closer to her.

"Five hundred Mark is what my Dad earns in
a month working in a machine factory. And it
doesn't buy a pair of shoes!" Karl fought hard to
hold back his tears.

"I don't know what to say," his aunt said after
moments of silence. She was thinking. Wrinkles
were etched on her forehead. "Maybe your uncle...I
could ask him to..."

"No, absolutely not!" Karl's head shot up. He
clenched his fists. "I will not accept a gift of

money from him or from you." More silence followed.

"Karl, my boy. Cheer up. Guess what?" Mrs. Huber shouted. She was clapping her hands rapidly.

Karl stared at his aunt with questioning in his eyes.

"You still have not received your Begrüssungsgeld, she exclaimed.

"Yes, that's right," Karl answered slowly. A weak smile began to thaw his frozen looks. He had heard that East Germans received one hundred Mark Begrüssungsgeld from a government office or a bank when entering West Germany.

"Let's go right now," his aunt encouraged him. "I have to do some shopping anyway. She took Karl by the arm and they headed for the garage.

The trip to downtown Feldhausen turned out to be both a disaster and a stroke of fortune. Karl came back home with no more than the fifty Mark he had received at the bank for his savings.

At City Hall a young clerk had turned down his request for Begrüssungsgeld. "I need to see your passport," he had demanded.

"I'm sorry, but I don't have it with me," Karl had replied.

"Then you will not be able to claim your money today," had been the reply. "But, here, take these free coupons: a hamburger with fries from McDonalds, a pass to the swimming pool, a pass for free public transportation, and a season ticket to attend the soccer games of Fortuna Feldhausen."

"I don't want any handouts. I don't need a season ticket. I'm going to play for Fortuna!"

He had said it, pushing the papers back across the counter. His own words had startled him. A sudden knowledge had struck him with full force while staring intently at the clerk: he would not accept alms. He would work and earn money for anything he needed.

Karl was sitting on his bed leafing through *Kreisblatt*, the local newspaper. He found the "Help Wanted" section. His eyes scanned the listings from "Aquarium Cleaner" to "Zoo Designer."

"That's for me!" Karl called out excitedly. His index finger traced a listing:

NEWSPAPER CARRIER NEEDED FOR EARLY MORNING

DELIVERIES. GOOD INCOME FOR DEPENDABLE PERSON

WITH TRANSPORTATION. CALL 876-0321.

That's it. No doubt. I get up early anyway. And I do have transportation, my legs. I'll earn money while getting a workout at the same time!

Karl went to the living room to make a phone call. He felt light-headed and very happy while dialing the number of the *Kreisblatt's* Circulation Department. Disappointment had set him free. He would depend on himself.

11

Mail

It was six o'clock in the morning on the second Tuesday after his arrival. Karl stood in front of the mail boxes of a small apartment building. He was looking at his list of newspaper subscribers. *Bruno, Hansi. Severens, Elizabeth and Willi, Hauptstrasse 17.* Karl's eyes moved across the names underneath the mail boxes. "Here they are," he exclaimed. In went two copies of the *Kreisblatt.*

Karl took a large canvas bag off of his shoulder. "Time for a break," he called out. A quick glance into his bag told him that about half of the papers already had new owners.

I have been very lucky lately. Karl sat down on the front steps. He raised his head high toward the clear sky. The air was cold and dry. Karl took a deep breath. *What a job I have! I get paid to keep in shape!* Karl slapped his thigh, jumped up, and made a dash toward the next mail box.

Later in the day, the Huber mail box handed Karl a wonderful surprise. There were two letters for him, one from his family and one from Monika.

"Dad's health is getting worse," his mother wrote at the end of her letter. "You know he had problems breathing. It's getting more painful every day. The poisons in the air are eating away at his lungs."

Dad has to get out of that awful factory! Karl spat through his teeth. *What a crime! Ruining his health! Why do they have to use all this dirty brown coal for energy?*

Karl finished reading and then reflected on his mother's letter. *It looks like they decided against moving to West Germany. They think they are already too old to start all over again. Mother is probably right. Things are not exactly as in paradise here, either.*

Karl hesitated to open Monika's letter. He enjoyed looking at the soft blue envelope. He liked the way she had written his name. His initials "K" and "N" were large and ornate. They reminded him of his favorite book of fairy tales. The first letters of each story in *Grimm's Fairy Tales* were also big and elaborate. Karl held Monika's letter with both hands. He closed his eyes and an image of a princess from one of Grimm's tales passed in front of them. *Too bad there are no more dragons or giants around. I would love to fight them all for Monika.*

"Coach Meierbär will have to do for a dragon if he won't let me play," he whispered with a smile. He opened Monika's letter. She invited Karl to come to her birthday party early in December.

The news sent a flood of elation through Karl's body. But the Huber family did not notice the sparkle that brightened Karl's eyes for the rest of the day.

12

Soccer Shoes

Mrs. Huber entered the room. "Rudi is going to Frankfurt today after school. Christmas shopping. Wouldn't you like to go with him?" she asked Karl.

"Yes, but..." Karl was tongue-tied, feeling the weight of his problem. He desperately needed a pair of soccer shoes and Christmas gifts for Monika, his family, and friends. However, he had very little money.

His aunt knew his worries. "Karl, I would be very hurt if you said no to this suggestion. You are earning money every morning. So, please take this and pay me back as soon as you get your pay check." Mrs. Huber took some bank notes out of her purse.

Karl thought for a moment. Then he answered, "It's a deal. Thank you very much. I'll pay you back as soon as I get my check."

"Boy, are you lucky I'm coming shopping with you," Rudi exclaimed. They were on the train to Frankfurt.

"Why?"

"Well. I know about soccer stuff — especially shoes, balls, jerseys — and soccer computer software, of course."

"Then you know where to go for soccer shoes?" Karl had his nose glued to the window. Snow flakes streaked past furiously.

"Not only that. But I know which shoes you must buy."

"Ohh.." Karl sighed.

"First of all you need a shoe with a 16 stud high density rubber outsole. It must have over-sized circumference lateral cleats which prevent your foot from roll-over. Then it must have a thermoplast heel for rear foot stability and..."

"Rudi, get serious, I don't..."

"Let me finish. Most important is the leather. It has to be kangaroo, by all means. Also, with a cambrella lining for..."

"Stop it, Rudi," Karl interrupted his cousin sharply. "I am not going to wear them for a soccer fashion show. I just want to get a pair of comfortable and durable soccer shoes."

Rudi threw up his arms. He almost shouted, "I guess you Ossis have little class. You like to wear ordinary shoes and drive dingy cars, like those Trabis and Wartburgs."

"Right. That's all we're able to get."

"Exactly, Karl. But now you're in West Germany. Here you can drive a Porsche, BMW, or Mercedes." Rudi spoke with an impassioned voice. "And above all, you can get the very tops in soccer shoes."

"I know, Rudi. I appreciate your suggestions. But I don't need a Porsche. I would settle for a Volkswagen."

"It sounds like you don't want my help," Rudi shouted, leaping up from his seat. "I have plenty of shopping to do for myself. I'll see you back home tonight." He darted toward the front of the train.

A pedestrian outside the Frankfurt train station gave Karl directions to the Zeil. He remembered his aunt saying that this was the major business district.

Karl walked down Kaiserstrasse, a broad avenue. He felt as if he were being pushed up and over a giant ant hill illuminated by flashing lights of all colors. The noise of honking car horns and screeching tires came from the left. Loud Christmas music escaping from the buildings to the right completed the assault on Karl's ears.

Things got worse inside Kaufhof, a large department store. Karl felt like a soccer ball trapped in the penalty area. A number of defenders attempted to boot him out of the danger zone, while a hoard of attackers tried to bury him in their opponent's goal.

Somehow Karl ended up on the escalator. He had the feeling of floating away from confusion and abuse toward a place of promise and surprise.

On the fourth floor Karl found himself in the sports department. *I am dreaming.* He had entered a chapter from his fairy tales.

Karl looked at balls, jerseys, sweats, hats, scarfs, and flags of all colors and from all teams imaginable. The red and black of the local professional club Eintracht Frankfurt dominated. But there were also things in the royal blue of Real Madrid and soccer merchandise in the black, white, and gold of the German National Team.

Karl stood open-mouthed. He gazed like a goldfish who had escaped his fish bowl and ended up in the shallow reef of the Red Sea.

Karl found the shelf with rows of nothing but soccer shoes. He turned a shoe around in his hand and stroked the soft leather. *How in the world can I decide which pair to buy?*

Pictures from shopping trips in East Germany flashed through his mind. When his mother had needed a pot, she bought the one brand that was available. When his father had needed a saw he bought the one that had a handle and a blade. It was the only model around. *Boy, how easy things used to be!*

Karl had made his decision. He left the department store with a white plastic bag holding his prized purchase. It had been impossible for him to buy gifts for his family or for Monika. *Too many things are shouting, "Buy me!" I'll be back some other time with a list of things to get.*

In the evening Karl paraded around the room wearing his new soccer shoes. They felt snug and comfortable. Karl thought of the way he had finally chosen them. He had his eyes closed and his nostrils wide open. The pungent smell, the pliable leather, the firm sole, and the soft padding for heel and ankle had made the decision for him. And above all, the shoes he was wearing seemed to make him a promise — in a mysterious way they assured him he would make deadly passes and guide blistering shots at the goal.

13

Practice

It was Thursday evening. Karl put all his soccer stuff in a sports bag. He looked at his watch and leapt to his feet. "Twenty to six, Rudi. Let's get going."

"Okay. We've got to hurry. I don't want to run a dozen laps for being late to practice."

Night had fallen. The floodlights bathed the stadium in a small valley at the bottom of a slope.

"Look at that field, Rudi!" Karl exclaimed. They had stopped running and Karl put his arm around his cousin's shoulder. "A giant carpet, green and sparkling, just waiting for us."

They hurried down the path. Karl stopped abruptly; his eyes opened wide. He stared at two figures moving down the hill to the right of the stadium. Long shadows followed their steps toward the gate. Karl's eyes followed the apparitions until they disappeared in the shadow of the main bleachers.

"What was that?" he shouted at Rudi.

"Those were the two Meierbärs, our coach and

his son Bruno. They live in the club house up on the hill."

"But what were they carrying on their shoulders?" Karl's voice came sputtering and filled with fear.

"What's the matter, Karl? They were carrying corner flags. We use them to make mini goals."

"I saw two 'Vopos'..." he started to explain but didn't complete his sentence. He realized that his cousin wouldn't understand. How could he share with Rudi the tormenting scenes engraved in his heart? To him those figures were not Mr. Meierbär and his son. Instead, he had seen two 'Vopos,' the hated East German police. For a second he had seen them walking along the Berlin Wall, rifles on their shoulders, ready to kill.

At the stadium gate they met the Meierbärs. The coach, a mountain of a man, dark and square, was planted inside the gate. He appeared to fill its entire frame. "You must be Rudi's cousin," he said, reaching for Karl's hand.

Karl felt a vise gripping his right hand. "Yes, Sir,. I am Karl Neumann. I am really looking forward to practice tonight."

"Sorry, but I have bad news for you. I thought it over. We can't use you." Coach Meierbär spoke without emotion.

Karl felt as if someone had just slugged him in the stomach. His mind went numb and his upper body caved in slightly. Then he came back with a weak reply, "But you said to my uncle I could..."

The coach cut him off. "Well, I changed my mind. We could have used a big, strong defender. Klaus is out for the season with a knee injury. But I can see that Mr. Huber is right. You're a lot smaller than..."

"But I can shoot. I'm fast. I can fight!" Karl cut in, yelling in desperation. "And here, look, here are my new soccer shoes!" Karl reached into his bag and stuck his shoes in Meierbär's face.

The coach went speechless and stared at Karl with frozen looks. Suddenly, Mr. Meierbär swiped at Karl's soccer shoes with his paw-like hand.

Karl pulled his shoes away and, with his other arm ready to strike, lunged at Rudi's coach.

Rudi and the coach's son reacted swiftly. Rudi grabbed Karl by the collar of his training suit while Bruno yelled, "You don't act like that around here, little Ossi."

Karl felt a sharp pull before tumbling backwards and crashing to the ground.

Slowly, Karl's head cleared. He opened his eyes. On top of the gate he read the sign FOR MEMBERS ONLY. Karl got up on his rubbery legs. Half falling, he stumbled along the stadium fence into the dark night.

14

Arrest

Karl woke up shivering. His back felt cold and wet from the moisture in the grass, but his head, resting on his soccer bag, had stayed dry. Above, stars struggled through the fog. At some distance ahead, dim lights outlined Fortuna Stadium.

The past events paraded through Karl's mind. Then, as if to shake himself free from the nightmarish encounter with the two Meierbärs, he jumped up and grabbed his bag. In search of warmth and comfort, Karl headed toward his uncle's house.

In bed at home sleep would not come. Conflicting feelings clashed in his heart. The thought of staying in the Huber house any longer became torturous. Rudi's snoring, from deep in his throat, sent shivers running down Karl's back. *What should I do?* Karl agonized.

What would Martin do now? Karl fixed his eyes on the rock up on the shelf. At last, he got up and reached for Martin Rock.

Martin, you wouldn't let them get away with it!

Not even a try-out! **For Members Only!** *If you had known that this could happen in the West, you would not have risked your life!* No way!" came a yell from deep inside Karl. "Down with the fence!"

Ten minutes later, Karl had finished packing. Quick steps carried him and his few belongings out of the house and back to the stadium entrance with its hateful sign. Out of the bag came Martin Rock. Blow after blow Karl brought it crashing down on the gate.

When the first daylight arrived Karl crawled through the hole he had carved out of the lock-wire fence inside the gate's frame. He put on his new soccer shoes. Then he chased about the field, ball at his feet.

Karl did not hear or see the police arrive. He had just drilled a shot into the net: a free kick over an imaginary wall of defenders, when one of the two police officers grabbed him by the shoulder.

"Please come along. We need to talk to you about trespassing and property damage."

Karl sat in the police station face to face with an officer. *I did what had to be done.* He felt strangely calm and at ease. *I can handle the consequences.*

"Karl Neumann, hmm," the young police officer said slowly. "Born in Wittenberg, East Germany. Staying with the Hubers." There was a pause and more drawn out "Hmms" followed while Karl kept nodding his head.

"Did you, by any chance, have an accident with a young bicyclist?" the police officer asked, raising his voice and leaning forward across his desk.

Karl waited until he met the officer's eyes. "Yes, Sir. I did."

The police officer got up and Karl noticed the warmth in his eyes when he came close. "Karl, I think we have a common acquaintance. You know Monika Sanchez, don't you?"

"I sure do." Karl's smile had widened into a big grin.

"I am Mr. Kuehn, Franz Kuehn," the tall, trim police officer introduced himself. He shook Karl's hand with obvious pleasure. "I am not only a police officer, but I am also the coach of Germania Burgholz."

"You are?" Karl replied open-mouthed.

Mr. Kuehn nodded. "Monika told me all about you."

"She did?"

"Yes. You certainly must have made quite an impression on her. She thinks that you're an excellent soccer player."

"I can play," Karl said after a pause. He felt a rush of blood invade his face.

Mr. Kuehn seemed to be momentarily lost in thought. Disappointment showed on his face. "Too bad you're playing for Fortuna already."

Karl shot back, "Oh, no! I am not playing on Meierbär's team." He kept shaking his head violently.

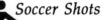

"You aren't? How come?" Mr. Kuehn was surprised.

"How come?" Karl was slow to answer. "I guess they don't want me. They won't even let me show them how I play." His voice was filled with bitterness.

"Did you say it was your cousin who pulled you down by the stadium gate?" Mr. Kuehn asked after Karl had filled him in on all the major events since leaving his family.

"Yeah, it was him. I guess he wanted to protect his coach. Rudi is okay, though. But I don't think he likes me."

Karl paused for a moment. Then he raised his voice and his eyes glared. "But Meierbär! He is a monster."

"I see you're upset - and with obvious reason." Karl sensed Mr. Kuehn's understanding. "But what are we going to do now?"

Silence followed. Mr. Kuehn paced the office while Karl stared at the ceiling with a strained neck and a tightened jaw.

"It seems to me that you don't want to go back to the Hubers," Mr. Kuehn finally remarked. He turned to Karl. "Am I right?"

"Yes."

There was more silence and Karl felt an awkward heaviness settling down in the room.

"Home. Karl, you always have a home: parents, friends, back in East Germany." Mr. Kuehn's voice was slow and deliberate.

Karl nodded. "Yes. And I am glad I do."

He paused, and then with sudden determination continued, "But now, now I want to be here! I want to play soccer here in West Germany. I want to see how far I can get and how good I can become."

Mr. Kuehn responded with a warm smile. "I live out in the country, in a small farm-house. Lots of animals. I am a bachelor. If you would like to, you could stay at my place for awhile. I would have to talk to your family first, though."

"They won't have any objections at all," Karl interjected eagerly.

Mr. Kuehn nodded. His eyes found Karl's. "And you would have to call the Hubers to explain the situation."

Karl jumped from his chair. "Sure, I'll talk to my aunt. She'll understand."

"It's all set then. You'll move in with me if your parents don't object. I am going to call them right now." Mr. Kuehn picked up the folder containing information on Karl and his family and left the room to use the phone in the office next door.

15

A New Home

Karl sat on the thick feather comforter which covered his bed in the guest room of Mr. Kuehn's old farmhouse. "Some three hundred years old," the proud owner had explained when they arrived yesterday. "I renovated it just two years ago." He had pointed at the black, shining wooden beam structure of his "Fachwerkhaus" when they were walking up to the front door.

My soccer ball sure looks lonely without Martin Rock. Karl's eyes took in the wall across from his bed. His ball sat prominently on top of a desk underneath a window facing the little orchard and the barnyard. The worn-out ball seemed very content to observe the lively activities outside. In front of a weathered barn a host of geese and chickens scampered about declaring war on each other and anything edible in sight.

Karl looked at his ball fondly. *He must be as ancient as this house. I wonder whether the government here pays subsidies for renovating worn-out balls.* He remembered Mr. Kuehn's explanation on how the West German Government helps to pay for keeping "historical things" like farm-houses in good condition.

Karl's mind took a leap and drew a picture of the near future. *As soon as the two countries reunite they'll have a field day rebuilding East Germany. Everything back home has gone to the dogs. But I doubt that my uncle will sell his Mercedes in order to help pay for collapsing bridges or rotten sewers.*

At the thought of his uncle, Karl jumped up. *I must call Aunt Gisela. She'll be worried to death not knowing why I did not come home last night.*

In the kitchen Karl found the phone and dialed his aunt's number. His heart fell as he heard Rudi's trumpeting voice, "Huber residence."

I sure didn't want to talk to him! An inner voice urged Karl to slam down the receiver. But as if hypnotized he heard himself say, "Oh, it's you Rudi."

"You, Karl? Are you calling from prison? We heard you were arrested yesterday morning."

"No, Rudi. Tell your mother I'm okay. I'm staying at Mr. Kuehn's place. I'll take care of things around the house, the animals,the fire-place. I also have to..."

"You're not going to play on his team, are you?" Rudi cut in half threatening.

"Well, maybe. I sure hope to. I feel I'll get a fair shot. Coach Kuehn is going to let me show that I can play."

"Well, you'll make a *big* mistake," Rudi admonished. "Kuehn is known for being too soft. He thinks he can *outplay* an opponent."

"I kind of like that idea. My style." Karl sounded excited.

Rudi conceded, "Well, Kuehn's Germania is not a bad team. They are able to push around some of the pussycats in our League. But we killed his team, ran 'em off the field, on their own ball park."

Karl closed his eyes for a second. He pictured his cousin's head swelling as he was singing the praise of Meierbär's team.

Then came his weak reply, "That was earlier in the season, Rudi. The second half is still to come. And after a short pause he added with regained confidence, "Anything can happen. We'll get another shot at your team."

"Yeah, sure, Karl."

Silence followed. Then Rudi spoke again. "Well, Good Luck anyway, Karl."

"Thanks a lot, Rudi," Karl replied, almost in shock at his cousin's good wish and soft tone of voice.

"And...I guess... well I am..."

"Yes, go on, Rudi."

"Well, I'm kind of sorry for what happened at the stadium with Meierbär. I pulled you back so you wouldn't get tangled up with coach and get hurt."

"Thanks, Rudi. I understand. No hard feelings. Tell your mom and dad that I called and let 'em know where I am staying."

 *Soccer Shots*

Karl poured cereal into a breakfast bowl while his mind mulled over the note Mr. Kuehn had left him before leaving for work early. *Wow, I'll be a busy boy today: feed chickens, clean stables, chop wood, wash dishes.*

Karl took a couple of deep breaths. He chased away the pictures of chores awaiting him. There were other, more pleasant events signaling their arrival: Monika's Birthday Party, meeting his new team, exploring the surrounding woods, and playing — playing lots of soccer.

Let's get to work! Karl jumped up from the kitchen table and headed for outside. At the back-entry door another note caught his eye. *Erst Arbeit, dann Spiel.* Karl smiled. Mr. Kuehn told him first to work, then to play. The note also mentioned that there was a small soccer field awaiting him behind the barn—after work.

16

Germania Burgholz

A surprisingly sunny afternoon on a Sunday early in December found Karl on his way to the Sanchez home. *Not a single cloud in the sky to spoil Monika's big day.* Karl was looking in amazement at the blue sky above him.

Monika opened the front door. Her face flashed a beaming smile.

Karl ran up to her. "Happy Birthday, Monika!"

"Thank you, Karl. It's great to see you again. I'm glad you were able to come." They hugged.

"Here, this is for you." Karl handed Monika a bouquet of flowers.

"Red roses! They are beautiful. Fifteen of them. How did you find out my age?"

"I asked. I called the Lord Mayor of Burgholz."

Monika laughed out loud.

Karl followed Monika into a spacious, modern living room. It was dressed up for the occasion. A host of balloons of all colors bobbed their huge heads against the ceiling. Strings of paper snakes stirred in the light breeze entering through an open window.

Streaks of sunlight danced among the dishes, snacks and flowers spread out on a massive table.

"Karl, sit down," Monika pointed to the leather sofa. "We can talk. You got here early."

"Of course, I want to be the first in line for all that delicious food." Karl smiled while his eyes swept across the large table. He sat down next to Monika.

"By the way, Monika, thanks for telling Coach Kuehn about me."

"Oh, sure. I just had the feeling you'd be able to help our team. I heard you moved into his house a few days ago."

"Yeah. Things are going great. I love to be around all those animals. It reminds me of home."

"Lots of work, I guess?"

"That's for sure. I earn my keep. In exchange for doing plenty of chores, Mr. Kuehn is paying for the damage I did. I think I'll get off easy. They won't put me in prison or deport me."

Monika smiled. "I wouldn't let them. We have a lot of great hiding places nearby in the forests. Caves, hollow trees. I even know of a cabin where a hermit used to live."

They looked at each other. Karl felt the warmth in Monika's eyes.

After a short while Monika spoke first. "Karl, tell me more about what happened at Fortuna Stadium. It caused quite an uproar. You demolished the gate, didn't you?"

"Yes, but in the process I smashed my Martin

Rock into pieces." Karl then told Monika about his brother and how he, Karl, had chiseled a chunk out of the Berlin Wall.

"It's too bad that it got broken," Monika exclaimed.

Karl nodded. "I can't believe it myself. That Concrete Beast slashing Berlin into two pieces is rock-solid. Probably the most perfect thing they ever built in East Germany. But even that masterpiece must have had some shoddy spots."

"I think it's coming down. All of it. I hear some American, some guy from Hollywood or Texas, maybe, is buying up the wall."

"I wouldn't be surprised, Monika. I don't know of anything the Americans couldn't turn into money. But I would just like a few pieces of my Martin Rock. Mr. Kuehn promised to drive me there soon to pick up what's left."

Monika's party lasted till late in the evening. Back home, Karl thought of all the new people he had met. *The Germania players are super. What characters! And "El Loco." What a joker!* Karl felt that he had hit it off well with Monika's brother.

All evening long Karl had listened to stories about Carlos, whom they called "El Loco" or the "Crazy One." Although playing as Germania's goalkeeper, Carlos had established quite a reputation as a field player. In two of his "excursions" into the opponent's field of play Carlos had scored goals. Mr. Kuehn called Carlos the "Higuita of Burgholz." This was an obvious reference to the

dazzling goalie of Colombia's National Soccer Team.

Wednesday, the first day of practice with Germania, had arrived. Karl shook hands with some of his new teammates: Carlos, Thomas, Willi, the captain, and Gerd, the fastest player on the team. Although it was cold, the ground frozen, and a thin layer of snow lay upon the field, fourteen Germania players in sky blue sweats were soon dashing about the field.

Mr. Kuehn kept practice simple. "Get out and play!" he yelled. "To the ball. Everybody back. Shoot!" Mr. Kuehn fired on his players for ninety minutes.

While the coach kept fanning the enthusiasm, Karl did not stop moving. His pin point passes found their targets. Loose balls in his vicinity were his booty. Shots on goal exploded from each of Karl's feet.

El Loco, playing for the opposing squad, definitely earned his title. Although he dove like a madman, Karl beat him three times with rocket shots low to the ground.

At the end of the practice Karl was surrounded by teammates in high spirits. "I'm glad you aren't playing center-forward for Fortuna," Carlos exclaimed with his hand on Karl's shoulder.

"Great game, Karl!" Willi congratulated him with a pat on the back.

"You're not going to leave this team or this

city!" Thomas added with a big grin on his face. Karl basked in his friends' well-wishing.

Mr. Kuehn came up to him when they entered the dressing-room. "Karl, you're on the team!" The coach looked at him warmly. A firm handshake said everything else.

17

Threats

Winter was losing its grip on nature. The days were getting longer. Crocuses and daffodils peaked through patches of snow, signaling the arrival of spring.

A few months back, Karl had enrolled in the Burgholz Johann Wolfgang von Goethe Gymnasium, the local high-school. He was walking tall in the halls and school grounds, among classmates, friends, and teachers. He was earning good grades in all of his classes, except for English. Two subjects, Biology and German, he studied with Monika. They sat next to each other in class and hung out during breaks. Often they were joined by Carlos and other Germania players. Their laughter filled the school grounds.

Karl walked tallest when he thought of soccer, the joy of playing and practicing with his teammates from Club Germania Burgholz. He felt pride when friends and even strangers mentioned the contributions he had made playing in the last eight games for his new club.

On a Saturday, early in April, Karl sat in the living room, reading the sports page of the *Kreisblatt*. For the third time he poured over this article:

Germania in Hunt for Title

Germania Burgholz is the surprise team of recent weeks. Trailing Fortuna Feldhausen by 5 points at the halfway mark of the season, Coach Kuehn's team is now only 1 point behind the leader. With two games to go, the showdown will most likely be on the final day of play when Fortuna hosts Germania. Assuming that both teams win their next game, Germania needs a victory for the title. Feldhausen will only need a tie for the championship.

Germania's impressive run on the title must be attributed to two players: goalkeeper Carlos Sanchez and forward Karl Neumann. Sanchez posted 6 shutouts in the last eight games and has been performing superbly. Neumann, a transfer from Lokomotive Wittenberg, is on a record-breaking scoring run. Since joining the team at the half way mark, Neumann has tallied sixteen goals. This puts him in second place behind Fortuna's Bruno Meierbär, who leads the league with eighteen goals.

With Sanchez and Neumann at their best, Fortuna will be in a dogfight for the title which had seemed only a formality a few short weeks ago. Both players, by the way, are being closely observed by scouts from the Bundesliga Club Eintracht Frankfurt.

Since the game between Fortuna and Germania will be a sure sellout, tickets should be purchased ahead of time at the stadium gate or at Fortuna's club office. It will also be shown live on local TV.

Karl could hardly believe his eyes. But there it was in black and white: his name was in the paper and Eintracht seemed to be interested in him. *What a game this is going to be! I can't wait to get back into Fortuna Stadium!*

The next day, Karl came home from school early in the afternoon. It was Thursday, two days before their game at Schlossheim. Walking up the driveway from the main road, he was absorbed in his thoughts. *That is a must-win game. If we don't win this weekend, we won't even need to show up in Feldhausen.*

Karl opened the mail box. He was hoping to find a letter from his parents or friends in East Germany. But there was only one envelope, an unusual looking one.

Bold black capital letters spelled out his name **KARL NEUMANN**.

Nothing else — no address, no sender. *Not even a stamp. This letter was hand-delivered!*

Karl went inside the house and sat down at the kitchen table. Apprehension clouded his face.

This is trouble! He pulled out a plain, brownish piece of paper.

A short sentence in large red letters stared in his face: **STOP PLAYING OR ELSE....**

A photo of a leg in a cast, cut from a magazine, was glued to the paper at the bottom of the page.

Karl took some deep breaths. *Just a short friendly message from Fortuna, no doubt.*

Karl was not able to shake himself free from his worries. In the evening he talked things over with Mr. Kuehn. He also told his coach of another incident at school some three or four weeks back. "One morning I opened my math book in class and a note dropped out. Same paper, same writing. **OSSI GO HOME** it said. I tried to put it out of my mind."

"We can't ignore these threats, Karl. This is serious. You and I need to deal with it." Mr. Kuehn wore a stern look while stroking his chin.

"What are we going to do, Coach?"

Mr. Kuehn stared into space before answering slowly, "As a police officer I should know, right? But I don't know. Not yet."

"Fortuna?" Karl raised his eyebrows and looked at his coach intently.

"I think you're right. The Fortuna gang is behind all this for sure. However, we've got to be patient and careful. So far, we have no evidence that they are the guilty ones."

Karl nodded. "I don't trust those guys, especially the two Meierbärs."

"I don't either, Karl. But you need to stop

worrying now and go to bed. You need a good night's sleep."

"I guess so." Karl got up and walked slowly toward his bedroom only to make a sudden turn before reaching the door.

"But what about the game in Schlossheim? The picture? The leg in the cast!" Karl's voice was filled with worry.

Mr. Kuehn came up to Karl and put his arm on his shoulder. "I have an answer for this. Absolutely! I already know how we will deal with this situation. Trust me Karl. You don't have to be concerned about the next game."

A trace of doubt still lingered on Karl's face when he asked, "What's the plan, Coach?"

"I will make a few changes for that game — changes in the lineup."

Karl looked puzzled. "What kind of changes?"

"I'm still working on the details. I will let you know when I get everything worked out."

"I am going to play, aren't I?"

"Yes, for sure, Karl. We need you. And we need to accomplish two goals." Mr. Kuehn paused for a moment. They looked into each other's eyes.

"First, you must leave the game without injury, and we must win. Somehow we will accomplish this. Then we'll deal with the Meierbärs and our next game."

Karl was satisfied. He said good night and went to bed. Sleep came quickly.

18

Away Game at Schlossheim

"Great job today, guys," Coach Kuehn praised his team. The Germania players had just settled down in the team's meeting room after the last practice before their crucial game. "Just super, you did exactly what we have to do on Saturday in Schlossheim."

"You mean like blasting the ball into the stands," Carlos joked, slapping Karl good-naturedly on the shoulder.

Karl remembered his misfired missile towards the end of their scrimmage. "No, Carlos, Coach is talking about taking dives but not *after* the shot has gone into the net."

The Germania players roared with laughter. Coach Kuehn held up both arms in an attempt to calm down his team. He could not suppress a smile, though. "Enough you two. This is serious. We've got quite a job in front of us. If we do it, we're off to Italy!"

"I already packed my suitcase, swimming trunks, suntan lotion, and the rest." It was 'El Loco' again who couldn't pass up an opportunity to make light of Mr. Kuehn's words.

The Germania coach tightened his jaw. Then his words came slowly and solemnly. "Mr. Sanchez, this is it." Coach Kuehn reached into his bag and pulled out a yellow card. He went up to Carlos and flashed it into his face. "Next time it's red and you're out of here — Adios, Hasta la Vista, amigo."

Karl noticed a smirk on Mr. Kuehn's face. Then he looked at his friend. Carlos had his eyes lowered and his bold lips were shut tight. He looked submissive as if saying , "Okay, Coach. That's it." Karl knew his friend wouldn't push his coach's tolerance button again — at least not any more tonight.

"I'll say it one more time — we need to win at Schlossheim if we want to battle Fortuna for the championship."

"Fortuna Stadium is already sold out. No way we're going to lose, Coach," Andre blurted out.

"Yes, I know Andre. But that doesn't mean Schlossheim won't show up, giving us the two points as a present. Like any other team, they have pride and want nothing more than to spoil our party."

"No doubt, guys," Willi said out loud, " They'll put up a fight! Last year we got our butts kicked at their place. We got to play smart, play **our** game."

"Right, Willi!" Coach Kuehn thanked his captain with a warm look and a nod. "And our game is ball possession, quick, accurate passing. They'll run at us like a herd of bulls. We'll not get into duels with their guys and risk injuries."

"Yeah, we worked at that all practice long. You never made such a big deal before about getting rid of the ball. Why now, Coach?" Gerd asked.

"Good question, Gerd. We have to take special precautions with this game. There is a very good reason. I am still working on the details. There will be a change in the lineup and you guys can't give them a chance to tackle you and injure you."

Although the Germania players pressed their coach to reveal more and to "stop acting so mysteriously," Coach Kuehn wouldn't say any more about his plans than he had already indicated to Karl earlier in the day.

After rehearsing the players' responsibilities for defending on set plays, the coach dismissed his team with a last reminder. "You'll get all the details before the game. For now, just make sure you'll be ready. You know what to eat and drink. And your shoes, cleaned and shined!"

All heads nodded obediently. Not even Carlos dared to crack a joke. Karl remembered more than one occasion when one of his teammates didn't play in a game because "the tools of his trade were not in working order." Mr. Kuehn had alluded to the dirty shoes a player was wearing for practice or a game.

Mr. Kuehn paused for a moment. Furrows crept up on his forehead. Then he went on, "Just two more things: Number One, you're going to be in bed by 10:30 tonight and tomorrow, you need to be rested and ready — that's the bottom line — the rest will take care of itself; Number Two: we'll leave from the clubhouse Saturday morning at nine, sharp."

Germania Burgholz kicked off against Schlossheim on Saturday. Karl sat on the bench next to Coach Kuehn.

"Why isn't Karl starting?" Coach Kuehn repeated, turning to one of the substitutes who had asked him. "My hunch is that Karl would be a very marked man today."

"What do you mean?" a number of voices asked.

"Like I said, guys, it's just a hunch," Mr. Kuehn replied while his eyes followed the action on the field. "And I'm not explaining my reasons again. You should have listened to me in the dressing room a little while ago."

Karl was still confused about Mr. Kuehn's plan. Thomas was on the field wearing Karl's jersey, number 9, and playing in midfield. Gerd had Thomas' position as left fullback. *As long as I get to play very soon, it's okay with me. Mr. Kuehn is a good coach. He knows what he is doing.*

"Look at Schlossheim's number 6!" Mr. Kuehn shouted excitedly, pointing at a very tall, muscular player on the opposing team. Karl saw him shadowing Thomas closely.

Then, all of a sudden Germania's bench players jumped up, throwing their arms in the air. "Get that guy out of here!" "What a vicious tackle!"

Yells of protest exploded from their mouths. Thomas was on the ground. He held his right ankle in pain. Schlossheim's number 6 had felled him with a two-footed tackle from behind. The referee was on top of the situation. The culprit was red-carded, sent off the field after receiving a stern talk.

Thomas hobbled to the sideline. Soon, the trainer had found that the injury, fortunately, wasn't as serious as everyone had suspected at first.

Coach Kuehn was extremely angry. His eyes flashed and he barked at Thomas. "What did I tell you? Play the ball quickly! No unnecessary dribbling! No unnecessary duels!"

Thomas sat on the bench, his chin on his chest. Karl knew that his teammate felt bad about ignoring the coach's instructions. *It's tough to forget what you have been doing all season long, especially if you're as good at dribbling as Thomas.* Karl saw pictures of his teammate as he ran circles around opponents in previous games.

"Karl, go in now!" Mr. Kuehn shouted after he had gotten the linesman's attention and the referee's signal. "Be patient. Stay back. And make your passes early. Do you understand?"

"Yes, Coach," Karl called back over his shoulder as he rushed onto the field.

It took Karl only a few minutes to get control of the game. Like a traffic cop he directed the action in midfield. His passes to the wing-players, Andre on the left, and Boris on the right, exposed Schlossheim's weakness. The opponent had positioned a wall of defenders in the middle. They were unable, however, to stop Germania's two crafty and speedy wingers. Again and again, Andre and Boris beat their defenders to the outside, attacked the endline, and then crossed the ball dangerously in front of the goal.

Karl's team went into the dressing room at halftime with the game in control and a 2:0 score to show for it. Karl had scored the first goal. He had played a wall-pass with Willi and shot unexpectedly. His bullet from some 25 yards away had found the lower right corner of the net. The second goal came right out of Mr. Kuehn's playbook. Boris had beaten his man to the endline, and his cross to the far-post was headed home by Andre.

Coach Kuehn was beaming as he made the rounds, dishing out compliments generously.

Carlos slapped Mr. Kuehn gently on the back and returned the favor. "Great plan, Coach! Their number 6 never found out who Karl was."

"Right," Mr. Kuehn replied. "He kept looking around for help, but everyone else on his team was in a fog as well."

"And the ref," Thomas chipped in. "Awesome. He really gave it to him after that brutal takedown."

"I had a word with the ref before the game," Mr. Kuehn explained. "After all the threats Karl received we knew fishy things were brewing."

The game ended 5:1. Karl had scored another

goal in the second half. His exuberance had gotten the better of him. He had started a solo run in his own half and after dribbling and feinting his way past an army of defenders he slid the ball underneath a diving keeper into the net.

"Great goal, just what we had planned for today!" Mr. Kuehn congratulated Karl after the game.

Karl noticed the twinkle in the eyes and the slight sarcasm in the voice of his coach. *Ende gut, alles gut.* He felt lucky things ended well and that he got away with a friendly reminder for not following his coach's instructions.

"Fortuna, here we come!" "A day as beautiful as today should never pass away!" Loud singing and laughing rocked the bus. The celebration and laughter didn't stop till the team bus pulled into the parking lot of the clubhouse. Inside, the party went on. The owner treated the team and their coach to refreshments and a hearty meal.

"I still have a question, Coach," Karl said when they were back home. "Why would that big number 6 want to stick me so bad? Schlossheim had little to gain from getting me out of the game."

"Well, in a way, you're right. They are out of the running for the title. But I know their coach. Like most of us, he wants to win all the time. Let's face it. You're our play-maker and top scorer. If you are out, they'll have a chance to upset us."

"Hmm," Karl contemplated. "You really think that was all?"

"To be quite frank with you, no. I had a hunch, Karl, nothing more. Meierbär and Klotz, Schlossheim's coach, are friends and one of a kind. You may draw your own conclusions from that, my boy."

"I understand what you're getting at. We need to be prepared for the worst next Saturday, don't you think so?"

"Absolutely, Karl. This was just the beginning. You know what's at stake for them."

"You mean, the trip to Italy?"

"Yes. Meierbär recently made public what you already heard way back, that the League Champion, players and coach, will get a trip to the World Cup in Italy, all expenses paid."

Karl's eyes grew big and his face glowed. "And the trophy, don't forget the trophy, and the party, the excitement, all of Burgholz going bananas..."

"Karl, stop it. No more of this nonsense. We'll have to be cool and clever."

"Yeah," Karl conceded with a deep sigh. "Fortuna is not going to wish us a nice trip to Italy and roll over dead before the game starts."

"It's not going to be easy, Karl. We have to be on our guard like never before."

19

Phone Calls

On Thursday morning, two days before the big game, Mrs. Huber was on the phone. "Karl, listen, my boy. Coach Meierbär was here last night. He and my husband talked for a long time. I overheard some things. I'm still a little confused, but ...."

"What's the matter, Aunt Gisela?" Karl broke in. "You sound very upset."

"Yes. I'm quite disturbed. They talked about you and your game last Saturday."

"So what. I can imagine they aren't very happy about our victory in Schlossheim."

"Not only that. Mr. Meierbär thought things would turn out quite differently, especially as you yourself are concerned."

"What exactly did he expect?"

"Karl, I'm in a real bind. I know something is very wrong, but I just can't speak out against ..." Mrs. Huber paused. Only short, quick breaths came over the wire.

"Aunt Gisela, it's all right. Thanks for being concerned about me. Mr. Kuehn and I are handling things just fine."

"I know, Karl. So far, you have. You dodged the bullet." Mrs. Huber had regained her composure. "But on Saturday, Karl, I don't know. Do you have to play?" Her voice was filled with worry.

"Of course, Aunt. We've all worked so hard for this moment. Nobody is going to stop me or my team."

"I knew you would say that. Just be careful, Karl. I am very concerned about you." The phone went dead.

In spite of his brave talk on the phone, Karl found himself somewhat shaken. The two sinister notes, the ordeal in Schlossheim, and his aunt's warning combined to trouble him.

It was getting late, and Karl decided to skip school. He went back to bed, pulled the blanket over his head, and fell asleep.

Karl woke up when the phone rang around two o'clock in the afternoon. "I didn't see you in school today. What's the matter? Are you sick?" He listened to Monika's worried voice.

"I don't know what's wrong with me, Monika. I just feel totally wiped out."

"Hard practice yesterday?"

"You can say that again. Coach ran us into the ground. Station training, one on ones, and shooting practice."

"That's good, I guess. If you can survive a practice like that, you'll be able to handle Fortuna easily."

"You'd make a great coach, Monika. You sound just like Mr. Kuehn."

Karl heard Monika giggle. Then she spoke in a serious tone. "Are you worried about the game, Karl?"

"I can't deny it, Monika. They are going to try and make life miserable for us."

"Especially for you, I'm afraid. I know what they tried to do to you in Schlossheim."

"You do?"

"Just rumors, of course. I hear what Carlos and my father say. You probably know more than I do."

"Not much. But I feel much better now. That sleep did me good."

"I'm glad, Karl. I can't wait till Saturday. We'll have three or four fan-busses loaded up for the game."

"Great! I'll make a goal for you, Monika."

"I know you'll play well. They can't stop you. I'll be cheering. Take care, Karl. I'll see you in school tomorrow."

20

Game Preparations

Lively music blasted from the stereo while Karl soaked in a hot bath. He was alone in the house. "I must leave at once, Karl," Mr. Kuehn had said last night. He had received a phone call right after their return from practice. "I'll call you tomorrow to let you know what's going on," he had said before leaving.

The last of Karl's worries evaporated together with the hot water from the bathtub. After a huge lunch, Aunt Gisela-style, Karl did his chores. He fed the animals, worked around the barn, and then cleaned up the kitchen.

"Now, to my soccer stuff," he said out loud, smiling to himself. His blue sweats, blue jersey, white shorts, and blue socks went into the washing machine and then into the dryer. Karl folded them and carefully put them into his bag, next to his shinguards.

Karl held his soccer shoes up to the light. *You guys have been doing the job so far. Saturday is the real test, though. Let's keep up the good work!* Karl replaced the old cleats with new ones. Coach

Kuehn's words from the team-meeting after yesterday's practice still rang in his ears. "Boys, check your cleats. The turf at Fortuna Stadium will be soft. Most likely there will be deep mud in both goal-mouths. Best of all, put in new 3/4 inch studs. Without good footing, we might as well pack up and go home."

Karl looked for the gift he had received from Monika, a pair of new blue shoelaces. Thinking of his girlfriend, he tore out the old laces and laced his shoes with the new ones. Then he proceeded to clean his shoes, going over every inch with saddle soap. Afterwards, his shoes received a generous coat of black shoe polish. The rigorous shine job that followed made the black leather glisten.

And now, a couple of balls of crumbled news-paper for you guys to stay in shape. Karl stuffed the paper into his shoes, stretching the leather as if it was in contact with his feet.

The ritual was coming to an end. Karl wrapped his shoes into a double layer of newspaper and gently placed them inside his soccer bag. He zipped the bag up and put it on top of a dresser by the door.

Later on in the day Karl was overcome by the urge to take a walk. He followed a trail through the meadow bordered by a forest farther up on the hill.

Karl's body absorbed the warmth of the sun. Spring's balmy, scented air filled his lungs. The boundless spirit of nature was contagious. *Life is terrific. Will I be able to stand it after we beat Fortuna?*

Karl was on his way back to the farmhouse. Humming his favorite tune, he stepped out from among the trees. An unexpected sight startled him. To the left of Mr. Kuehn's house, a cloud of dust rose. Seconds later, a car emerged from it. Burning rubber, it roared onto the main road. Now in full view, the gleaming fiery red car sped away.

Who could that have been? Karl felt alarmed. In stride with his pounding heart he rushed down the hill.

Inside the house, Karl did not notice anything suspicious. *Still, I should have locked the front door before going out for my walk.* For a long time he felt a pang of guilt at his carelessness as he kept looking about the house slightly ill at ease.

The phone rang. Mr. Kuehn was on the line. "Why did you have to go all the way to Berlin?" Karl responded in surprise to his coach's initial words.

"I had to respond to an emergency. That's all I can tell you, Karl."

"But what about the game on Saturday?"

"Don't worry. I should be back in time. I already talked things over with Mr. Sanchez. He'll take care of the team until I see you. Everything okay?"

Karl related the strange incident that had just occurred as he returned from his walk.

"Hmm, very, very strange," Mr. Kuehn mused. "Did you say 'bright red car'?"

"Yes, fiery red."

"Karl, be careful. Lock the doors. Call Mr. Sanchez if you run into any problems."

"Okay, I will."

"I don't know what to make of this," Mr. Kuehn said gravely. "You know, red is Fortuna's team color. And practically everybody in Feldhausen drives a shiny red car."

"I know, Coach," Karl replied with a deep sigh.

"But don't worry, Karl. I'll do my best to be back on time. Go to bed now. It's almost 11 o'clock."

That fiery red glare. I have seen it before! Karl's mind was troubled. He tried to figure out what the next day would bring. The red shooting stars dashing wildly in front of his closed eyes held no answer or comfort and kept sleep away for a long time.

21

Shocking Discovery

The hour of the Championship Game was approaching. Thousands of Fortuna supporters were already inside the stadium. They waved red and white flags, pounded drums, and blared trumpets. Outside, lines grew longer and longer in front of the ticket offices and the entrance gates.

The Germania players stepped out of the team bus into an ocean of blue, fans wearing sky-blue hats, sky-blue scarfs, sky- blue jackets and swinging blue and white flags.

"Karl, tear it up!" a young female teenager from Burgholz shouted. She ran up to Karl and slapped his back good-naturedly.

"Just watch," Karl shouted back with a big grin on his face. "Keep up the noise!"

The team fought their way through the crowd of admirers. Some of the players signed autographs, shook hands with friends from school, or had a quick word with a supporter.

"Get in here! Cut out the hype!" Karl heard Mr. Kuehn bellow from the locker room entrance.

"Boy, Coach is nervous. Look at him freaking out," Carlos remarked.

"He sure is intense" Karl answered.

"But I'm glad he made it back. My father would have been a total wreck if he had to coach us today." Carlos sighed with relief.

Inside the locker room Mr. Kuehn was all business. "This is it, guys. Listen carefully!" Mr. Kuehn paused. His head moved around the half-circle. He found the eyes of every player. "I want you to be dressed in fifteen minutes. Then we'll be out on the field about half an hour before kick-off. Willi, you're the captain. Act like one. You know the warm-up routine. Take charge."

"Got it, Coach. We'll be ready," Germania's sweeper responded.

"Move around, work up a little sweat, stretch well. Then five against two, in two groups. Pass, move, talk. And the two guys in the middle, all-out pressure on the ball. Then you're back in here for last-minute instructions."

"Let's do it!" they yelled, more or less in unison.

"My shoes!" A shout pierced the muted buzz of game preparations. "My shoes are gone!" Karl screamed in agony.

Mr. Kuehn rushed toward the corner where Karl was getting dressed. "Karl, what are you saying?" Coach Kuehn's face had turned ash-gray.

Karl stood frozen stiff. His mouth was wide open. He gazed at a large potato in his hand. "My shoes are gone," he stammered.

Mr. Kuehn saw the potato and instantly realized what had happened. "Somebody stole your shoes and replaced them with this," he said unwrapping a second potato from Karl's bag.

By now, all of the players were in Karl's corner and wanted to know what was going on.

"We've got a problem. I'll take care of it. Willi, you..."

Mr. Kuehn did not finish his sentence. Carlos broke out into wild laughter. Karl's hangdog look, his rigid posture, and two arms attached to potatoes, instead of hands, was too much for him.

Carlos' sense of humor was infectious; waves of laughter spread through the team.

"Stop it!" Mr. Kuehn yelled. "This is no laughing matter. Willi, take the guys out. R-A-U-S! Out with you right now, I said!"

Karl and Mr. Kuehn were alone in the locker room. "Karl, we'll come up with another pair. You've got to play."

"But how?" Karl's voice trembled.

"I'll send Mr. Sanchez to Sporthaus Meister. Stores are closed by now, but maybe someone is still there."

"That would take forever," Karl replied without much hope.

"We'll try it. You wear size nine, right?"

"Eight and a half, Coach."

"Okay, that's Plan One. Plan Two: Christian, Thomas, and Fritz are our subs; you'll try on their shoes."

None of his teammates' shoes fit. They were all far too big. Karl fought to hold back his tears.

"Karl, put on another pair of socks and let's put some crumbled up newspaper into the tips of the shoes. That might work. At halftime, at the latest, Mr. Sanchez will be back with a new pair," Mr. Kuehn said cheerfully.

Karl wore Christian's shoes. He stumbled onto the field with a far-away look. He did not hear the roar from the east side of the stadium where their supporters chanted, "GERMANIA, GERMANIA" and welcomed the team's entrance with banners and flag-waving.

My God, how can I run, or dribble, or shoot, if I can't even walk straight? Karl felt seized by panic. An event from years ago went through his mind. He wore his grandfather's clothes — a pair of glossy black shoes, three sizes too big, a black suit, a black tie. Everything reeked of mildew and mothballs. It was the gray, gloomy day when he walked behind his brother's coffin.

22

Kickoff

The referee blew the whistle to signal Germania's funeral. Fortuna had won the coin toss and kicked off. Seconds later the stadium exploded. The Fortuna fans in the covered grandstand rose to their feet in wild cheers. Their team had scored. A long-range shot by Bruno Meierbär had blasted over Carlos' head into the net. El Loco had been parading around at the edge of the penalty box waving to his fans when Meierbär had pulled the trigger.

Germania was being buried alive. Waves of attacks came down upon their goal-area. Fortuna played like never before while Germania was out-played and out-hustled. They lost every battle for a loose ball and were run off the ball when they had it momentarily.

"You're not going to touch the ball today," Meierbär Junior hissed, beating Karl to the ball once again.

Coach Kuehn looked at the horror-show in agony. He frantically waved both arms back and forth in an attempt to get Karl's attention. Finally, Karl noticed his coach and came over toward the sideline.

"Karl, stay here a minute. Relax. Our defense is weathering the storm. Be ready for a counterattack."

Karl understood and remained near the chalkline. Neither Rudi, nor any of the Fortuna players paid any attention to him. Within the span of minutes, Carlos made four or five superb saves; two shots were cleared off the line by Andre, who had come all the way back from his forward position to help his team in distress. In anguish and total disbelief, Karl looked helplessly at the onslaught.

And indeed, Coach was right. The storm died down. Germania started a promising attack of its own. Willi beat Fortuna's burly red-headed midfielder and dribbled the ball over the midfield line. With a sudden sprint, Karl demanded the pass into open space on the wing. But at the very moment he was about to collect Willi's picture perfect through pass, a violent kick to his right leg brought him crashing down.

Karl screamed in pain and reached for his leg. A storm of protest rose from the visitor's bleachers while Coach Kuehn and a trainer charged onto the field.

Karl was put on a stretcher and carried to the sideline. The culprit, Fortuna's left fullback, received a yellow card, and the game went on.

Mr. Kuehn had not sent in a replacement for Karl. "I know, I'm taking a gamble. But if I substitute you now, Karl, you won't be able to come back. I hope you'll be all right. You've got to be!" Germania continued the game with ten players.

23

Fortuna's Locker Room

"Yes, of course. The whole works!" A voice shouted excitedly on the phone at the far end of the locker room. "And the champagne, the five kegs of beer, the bratwurst, ribs, sauerkraut. Get everything ready. And the band. Have it over here in 45 minutes. The championship is in the bag!"

Karl recognized the voice of the man who had finished his phone conversation and who was approaching him now.

"Oh, it's you, Karl," Coach Meierbär feigned surprise. "You couldn't take a little hint? Had to play today, or rather, try to." A nasty smirk played on his lips.

"Rat!" Karl hissed through his teeth inaudibly.

"By the way, gentlemen, this is the home team's locker room. How did you get in here?" Coach Meierbär turned to Germania's team doctor.

"Oh, it is?" the doctor replied. "Sorry, we had no idea. The door was open, and we just came in."

"I see," Meierbär replied with a snort. "Actu-

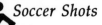

ally, no harm done. As long as you're out of here by halftime, in about ten minutes."

While the doctor checked his leg, Karl's eyes, grim and filled with pain, trailed Meierbär's hated frame. A minute later the door opened and Karl's eyes grew wide to a surprising sight: Monika stepped into the room.

Karl covered his face with both hands as if to hide the shame of his dreadful performance from his girlfriend. Stealing a look through spread fingers Karl saw her pacing about nervously in the unfamiliar environment.

By chance, Monika found herself in front of a bench filled with a row of Fortuna sports bags. All of a sudden, her eyes bulged. She stared at a red soccer bag with two laces dangling out of it. "What are these blue laces doing in a red Fortuna bag?" she wondered. She rushed to the bag and pulled on the partially opened zipper. "Those are the exact same laces I gave to Karl. A Fortuna player wouldn't wear them. How did they get on these shoes?"

Monika's eyes flashed wild with the half-grasp of an enormous discovery. She glanced about the room and found the trainer's bench where the doctor was wrapping Karl's ankle.

Monika picked up the shoe the doctor had removed from Karl's foot. "Strange, very strange," she thought. "Those shoes are old, the leather is cracked, they're filled with crumbled newspaper."

"Karl, I've got your shoes! Here they are! I

found them in that bag over there!" Monika screamed when the answer to the mystery had fully fleshed out in her mind.

"What are you saying, Monika?" Karl withdrew his hands from his face. He wore a look of total disbelief. "My shoes? Impossible!"

"No! Take them!" Monika handed Karl his shoes.

"Hey, these are my shoes!" Karl jumped up from the trainer's bench. His face was all smiles. "Monika, you're an angel!" Karl wrapped his arms around his girlfriend, threw her up in the air and gently caught her on the way back down.

Karl looked down at his soccer shoes as he hurried to his team's locker room. *I am myself again! What a feeling! Incredible!* The doctor had wrapped the ankle and somehow numbed the pain. It was no more than a nasty bruise.

Germania was downcast. The locker room was quiet and most sat with their heads in their hands.

"Hey, guys. It's me. Karl. I got my shoes back. I'm reborn." Karl shouted upon entering.

"Great, Karl," Willi replied. "But we're getting our butts kicked. We're down, two zip."

"So what? I got my shoes back. The second half is a new game."

"Karl is right, boys." Mr. Kuehn said. He tried hard to sound confident. "We can do it. There is plenty of time."

"Right on," Carlos added. "I'll stop waving to my fans and we'll shut 'em out this half. And you guys make three goals. Hey, it wouldn't be the first time."

Karl walked around, encouraging his teammates. Slowly his enthusiasm caught on. They huddled together and promised each other to fight like never before.

"Let's do it! I want to go to Italy and see Germany win the World Cup!" Carlos yelled as they scrambled out the door.

24

Second Half

Bruno Meierbär noticed the blue laces on Karl's shoes. The big guy's heart dropped into his shorts. He did not recover from his shock for the duration of the second half. Instead of breathing down Karl's back, he found himself trailing Karl by yards.

Some fifteen minutes into the period it happened. Karl chest-trapped a clearance by a Fortuna defender. He dribbled sideways, creating space for himself and giving his teammates time to run into open space. Suddenly, he reversed direction, getting past an opponent. Karl found open space in front of him and covered it in seconds. Two defenders rushed him.

Karl's soft through pass toward the penalty arc found Andre all by himself. He controlled the ball, turned, and released a shot with his right instep. Fortuna's goalie had rushed out of his goal to narrow the angle. Diving to his left, he managed to get a finger on the ball. But in vain. The ball was in the net, and the score was 2:1.

The Germania players mobbed their scorer, and the fans erupted on the east bleachers.

Both the players and the fans had tasted blood. Karl and his friends put the Fortuna goal under siege. Rudi, Bruno Meierbär, and practically every Fortuna player were back on defense. An impenetrable barricade cut off Germania's path to goal and victory.

Only twenty minutes were remaining. "Come on!" Willi yelled in desperation. "We need two more goals."

"The wings, play over the wings! Andre, stay wide!" Mr. Kuehn screamed, pacing the sidelines frantically. The ball came to Gerd on the left wing. He faked to the inside, cut to the outside, past his opponent, and then dashed toward the Fortuna goal. However, before Gerd was able to cross the ball, one of the countless defenders met him and tackled the ball over the endline.

The referee signaled a corner kick. Karl was already on the spot and made a run at the ball. He looked up and stopped his approach. He saw El Loco sprinting toward Fortuna's goal. He had his arm stretched high up in the air to get Karl's attention.

This can't be true! But he'll get the ball! Karl backed up to take a longer run at the ball.

Carlos was wide open. He connected with Karl's long, curving cross. A tremendous volley blasted through the wall of defenders and exploded in the net. The score was 2:2.

"TOR ! TOR!" The Germania fans went wild and Carlos was mugged by blue jerseys.

"Stop the celebration! Back!" Mr. Kuehn yelled

at the top of his lungs. Let's get the ball right back. He held one hand, fingers spread wide, high up in the air.

Karl knew what the signal meant. "We've got five minutes," he shouted at his teammates. "We can do it!"

Three, then four blue jerseys were on top of Rudi when he tried to control the kickoff. They stripped him of the ball and advanced it toward goal. Fortuna panicked. The shame of having been scored on by a goalkeeper had broken their spirit completely. Screaming at each other, they slashed at ball and opponent wildly.

With two minutes to go, Karl stole the ball from Bruno Meierbär. He gracefully stepped over Bruno's leg which desperately tried to tackle the ball away from him. Karl cleverly evaded another would-be tackler and then raced toward the Fortuna goal. Suddenly he was on the ground. Rudi had been waiting for him. A perfectly executed body block, football style, had sent him sprawling onto the muddy turf.

The referee called for a free kick and yellow-carded Rudi. Karl was still on the ground. He had crashed full speed into his cousin's huge shoulder.

Karl closed his eyes and took deep breaths. *This is it! This is the championship for us!* During the next few seconds, he visualized the shot he was going to take.

Karl got up slowly. Carlos, Willi, and a number of teammates stood around him. "Here is the ball," Carlos said. "Now, do to the Fortuna keeper what you have done to me a million times in practice."

Karl nodded and smiled. He placed the ball firmly on a smooth part of the ground. He stepped back and looked up. He faced the wall of eight players. Somehow, he looked right through them. He saw only the ball in front and the goal in the background.

The referee's whistle pierced the tension. Karl still paused, breathing deeply. Then he rushed forward. Karl's right foot struck the ball with all of his power concentrated on his instep. The ball swerved up and over the wall before crashing into the upper right corner of the net. 3:2.

The red wall of defenders crumbled to their knees. Karl, his face filled with ecstasy, stood with his hands high up in the air.

Bedlam followed. While the Germania players piled on top of Karl, the fans charged on the field. They screamed and hugged everybody in sight.

After order was restored, the game was over shortly. Carlos, unmolested by any Fortuna player, dribbled the ball around his penalty box and killed the last few seconds.

25

Final Whistle

The final whistle sounded. Carlos held on to the game ball. Germania had won the championship.

Players and fans were on their victory lap. Willi, the captain, led the pack, holding the trophy over his head. Mr. Kuehn was on Karl's side. "Karl, super job! What a comeback! What a shot!"

Coming around the last turn, Karl ran into Monika's arms. "I am so happy, Karl. Great game! That's the best you ever played!" Monika jumped up and down after the embrace.

"Thanks, Monika. You found my shoes. Without them we would have been buried today. That goal was for you."

Monika blushed slightly and reached into her jacket pocket. "Karl, stand still a minute. I have something for you." She opened a little box and took out a necklace.

Karl took it from her hands, studying it carefully. Small concrete chips, with holes drilled in the middle, were threaded on a thin leather string. "It couldn't be..." Karl's voice trailed off.

"Yes, it is Karl. I picked it up at the gate, after your demolition spree."

Karl, with his eyes glazed, looked at the necklace made with pieces from his beloved Martin Rock. Then, no longer fighting back his tears, he hugged Monika.

"Mr. Neumann. Congratulations. Very fine game." Karl shook hands with the gentleman dressed in an expensive looking suit. "I am Mr. Schmidt, I'm a scout for the Bundesliga club Eintracht Frankfurt."

"You are?"

"Yes. I've already talked to Carlos Sanchez. We would like to invite both of you to some training sessions. Here is my card. I will contact you again soon. I hope you're interested."

"I think, I am... I mean, of course," Karl stammered, still slightly dazed.

The next day, back at Mr. Kuehn's place Karl was talking on the phone. His aunt had called. "Thank you, Aunt. I am glad you're happy for me," Karl replied to Mrs. Huber's congratulations.

"Well, of course we celebrated! All of Burgholz was going bananas; we didn't stop dancing, singing, eating and drinking till late into the night."

Then Karl listened intently. He wore a serious look. "Of course I believe you, Aunt. I know it was all of the Meierbärs' doing. Sure, Rudi and my uncle wanted to win, just as badly as we did. But they wouldn't want to hurt me or steal my shoes."

Karl's face brightened as he continued to listen to his aunt.

"Cheesecake? Monika? I can eat two pieces of your delicious homemade cheesecake and I can bring Monika along?"

Karl listened to his aunt's explanations. "Aunt, you got a deal. Monika and I will come over for coffee and cake next Sunday."

Glossary

A

Adidas — German manufacturer of sports merchandise.

B

Begrüssungsgeld — "Welcome Money." East Germans received a gift of 100 Mark when they entered West Germany—or officially Bundesrepublik Deutschland — after unification in 1989.

Berlin — the former capital of Prussia and Germany. It was divided into East and West Berlin in 1945. Once again, it will be the capital of a united Germany.

Berlin Wall, The — and impenetrable barbed wire fences, 103 miles long, were built in 1961 by East Germany. These structures surrounded all of West Berlin and aimed at stopping the flood of citizens escaping East Germany to the free West. More than 100 people were killed in Berlin alone, trying to overcome this fearful obstacle.

Bratwurst — popular German link sausage. Germans like to eat it with a roll and mustard at fast food places, athletic events, parties, etc.

Bundesliga — the top professional German soccer league.

Bundi — an informal term referring to a citizen of the Bundesrepublik, the Federal Republic of Germany.

C

Communist Propaganda — opinions, doctrines held

in high esteem by a country or people believing in joint ownership of resources and a "classless society." The results have been lack of personal freedom and a modest standard of living.

D

DM — Deutsche Mark. The currency of the former Federal Republik. It remains the currency of the united Germany.

DDR — Deutsche Demokratische Republik, German Democratic Republic, also informally referred to as "East Germany."

E

Eintracht — United. The short version of Eintracht Frankfurt, a top club of the Bundesliga.

F

Fachwerkhaus — "Half-Timbered House." Historic, many centuries old homes. The German Government provides subsidies for their upkeep.

Feldhausen — an imaginary small city, near Franfurt am Main in the state of "Hessen."

Frankfurt — or Frankfurt am Main, Frankfurt on the river Main is a major city in central Germany. It is one of the leading business and banking centers in Europe.

Frankfurters — a pair of slender sausages or "hot dogs." Inhabitants of Frankfurt are also called *Frankfurter.*

G

Goethe, Johann Wolfgang von — famous German poet and dramatist.

Gymnasium — German for *high school.*

H

Haessler, Thomas — professional and national team player.

KJS — Kinder und Jugend Sportschule. Children and Youth Sports Academy of the DDR. High-powered training centers for promising young athletes.

Kreisblatt — *District Paper:* name for a regional newspaper.

L

Littbarski, Pierre — professional and national team player.

M

Mercedes — brand name and manufacturer of German luxury cars.

N

Nein — German for *no.*

O

Ossi — refers to a citizen of East (Ost) Germany. Depending on usage the term may have derogatory or endearing qualities.

P

Paella — name of famous Spanish food.

S

Schnitzel — often *Wiener Schnitzel.* A breaded veal cutlet, popular in all the German-speaking countries.

Strasse der Freiheit — Street of Freedom.

 *Soccer Shots*

T

Trabi — short for *Trabant,* the popular sputtering two-stroke automobile built in East Germany.

Tor — German for *goal.*

V

Volkswagen — *People's Car,* name of popular West German car and far more modest than the luxury cars of BMW, Mercedes or Audi.

Vopo — short for *Volkspolizei,* name of the East German police force.

Voeller, Rudi — well-known professional and national team player.

W

Wessie — refers to a person from West Germany.

Wittenberg — city in former East Germany; the site of Martin Luther's challenge of the Roman Catholic Church.

Germany Before Unification

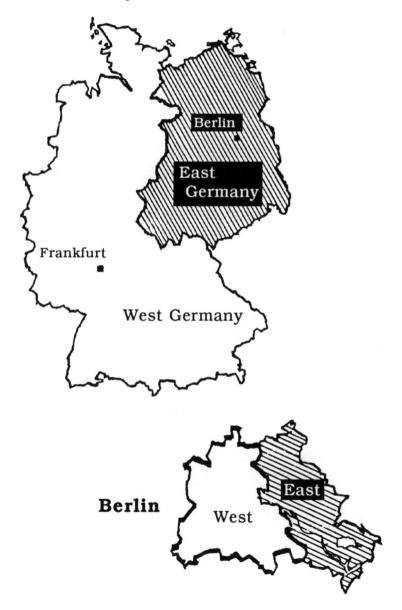

Soccer Shots is available
wherever you buy books
or
Order from:

Pacific Soccer School
1721 22nd Avenue
Forest Grove, OR 97116

Send check or money order for $10.95 per copy plus $2 for shipping and handling.

Please inquire about discounts for order of five books or more.

Allow 4 - 6 weeks for delivery.